# SHORT, NOT SO SWEET

*By*

*Vaughn Phelps*

I0683431

V. I. P.
Publishers

# *Short stories with a bite!*

Short Stories don't need to end with a statement. They might end with a question.   The protagonist need not be a good guy.

*This is an acknowledgement of all the help I've received from the many Support groups that gave critiques, all the Critique groups that gave support, the friends who said "That's not funny." And the contest judges who disagreed and awarded them placement.*

What I see as tongue in cheek, others often label hoof-in-mouth.

First Publication 2011 By Vaughn Phelps.

COPYRIGHT-2011
ISBN 978-0-9838938-1-3
Published in America by
V. I. P.
P.O. Box #911
Twin Falls, Idaho 83303-911

Also by Vaughn Phelps
SHORT, BUT SWEET

Other books soon to follow:
HEADS OR TALES,
STORIES THE C.I.A. COULDN'T STOP,
I TOLD YOU TO CHECK YOUR
PARACHUTE BEFORE WE JUMPED

# INTRODUCTION
## SHORT, NOT SO SWEET

By Vaughn Phelps
A.K.A. E.A.Po, Stephen Louis Robertson, William
Shakasteer, Oh! Henry and Burnt Harte.

Whenever a Gershwin or Cole Porter show tune is played, most people want to sing along. Remembering the lyrics is not a problem because all the words seem to fit naturally. In a Flash Short Story there's no place for anything that doesn't advance the plot or clarify the characters.

As originally conceived, all my happy ending stories would go into my first book and I'd save all the others for this one. In real life it was just boring that way. If you can predict the next story based on the last story, why continue? Anyway, that's why you'll find historical creative non-fiction, essays, monographs, fiction and of course, some—"swallow your plug of tobacco" total nonsense.

#

*"I'd love to write the music for any of these stories when ever they're made into films." G. Gershwin.*

#

# BOOK 2
# SHORT, NOT SO SWEET
## TABLE OF CONTENTS

# BOOK 2
# SHORT, NOT SO SWEET

## 1-ABANDON HOPE, ALL YE WHO ENTER HERE

Laura climbs off the bus with a worn and stained suitcase. The town looks even smaller than the map indicated. One oil-puddled, single-pump gas station, one paint-starved restaurant, a corrugated blacksmith's shed, single clapboard livery stable, an understandably lonely motel with the look of total abandonment. Three saloons show the only signs of life. It's an inhabited ghost town she'd ever not wanted to see. With a sigh, she trudges the dusty road, heading for the restaurant (that's being generous). Not the best; but the only, so by popular vote it's allowed to be. The screen door slams shut behind her as if some power is closing the door to the world on her. Bravely she slumps onto one of the mismatched, ripped and taped counter stools.

"Coffee, please."

The woman behind the counter pours hot black liquid into a chipped mug and shuffles forward to set it before her. With no word of greeting, she studies the girl as a scientist viewing an unrecorded species. The girl seems unrattled by this intrusive and impolite staring.

"You just left the Salt Lake bus. That all the luggage ya got? Must not be plannin' on stayin' long."

"Well, I…"

"This as far as your money took ya?"

The girl sips coffee and stares into its black depth. Finally, straightening her back, she returns the intensive look of her inquisitor.

"I figured I could get a job here and…"

She can't hold eye contact.

"Can you weld, fix cars, tend horses or run drinks for a bunch o' mangy galoots?"

"No.   At least I've never done any of those things, but I'm willing to learn."

"Don't matter none.   Ain't none o' them jobs available anyways."

"Oh."

"Looks like ya need it, so you can work here.  I'm modernizin' the motel.  I own both these dumps.  Regular Donald Trump of Eden, Idaho, ya might say.   Fifteen bucks a day, meals, and you can stay at the motel no charge.  Whatcha say?"

"I really appreciate it, I don't know what I'd have done if…"

"Ah, don't start bawllin and tellin' me your life story.  I already figured your man done ya wrong and you just up an' skedaddled.   If that ain't right, it'll be close enough.  I'm Abigale.  You go on down and pick yerself out a room, none o' the doors is locked.   Then come back here and have a meal.  You start work at six A.M.   The local turd kickers got nothing better to do so they come in here ta do it and they like to get an early start."

"Thanks so much.  My name is Laura Flynn."

She finishes her coffee, takes her bag and heads for the motel fifty yards down the road.   Room number 13 seems fatefully to call out to her.  It's a 1930's style cabin, obviously not one of the remodeled units.  But for the dust that blows in through the gap under the door, it's livable.

\* \* \* \* \* \*

Pre-dawn, she starts the next day as a one-woman restaurateur.  The men enter by twos and threes.   They bring with them the smell of mud and cows, and when they leave they don't take it with them. The flea-bitten bunch are all dressed as if by the same costumer; worn calico shirts, stained bib overalls and greasy ball caps advertising tractors, sporting goods, seed distributors and truck parts.

As a man, they make sexist (but complimentary) remarks about the welcome addition behind the counter. Laura accepts their comments with a shy smile, but without the obviously expected retort. Their average age is at least sixty with belt sizes about the same.

She's surprised that orders are soon flying for biscuits and gravy, eggs and bacon, flapjacks, oatmeal, grits, hash browns and mounds of toast. That she is an untrained chef or even has a nodding acquaintance with cooking is quickly evident. She serves burned flapjacks, cold gravy over hard biscuits, runny eggs and greasy bacon and gets only smiles and thank you, maams. The men unanimously show no anxiety over the delay in getting their food. They even refill their own coffees.

The apron she wears over her thin cotton dress is overlapped twice and held in place with a couple of clothespins. When the first wave of the laughing, joking, tobacco chewing, backslapping outdoor types finally leave, she slumps onto a rickety chair. Abigale comes in to make her own lunch.

"How's your first day goin'? I figured you'd get on okay with ground-pounders what still call theyselves cowboys."

"Well, I ruined a lot of food and was shocked when nobody sent anything back or refused to pay and most plates were scraped clean and I see why you make coffee ten gallons at a time."

11

"They's a pretty raunchy bunch with me, but they can behave 'round a lady.   I figured you'd have no real problems with 'em."

The afternoon goes slower and with less stress. Most of the men are satisfied with simple grilled cheese or tuna sandwiches and bags of chips.   The only woman customer, the wife of the blacksmith, orders PB&J and tea.

* * * * * *

Her third day goes better, with less burned food; eggs that try to hold together and warm gravy over room temperature biscuits.   Her tips have increased, but then tipping is a new experience for these men.   Together they learn as she familiarizes herself with transitioning raw food into cooked, food.   Her efforts never look like anything you'd see in a cookbook.   Not even one from Devil's Island.

A tall, well-built man of about thirty-five, dressed like he's heading for the rodeo ring enters, plunks his sweat-stained Stetson down on the counter and takes a seat before spotting Laura.   The smile that comes naturally splits his face into eyes and nose untouched by sunlight and mahogany colored mouth, chin and neck. His crows-footed eyes sparkle even in the dim light from the flyspecked light fixtures.

"Coffee and whatever's your specialty please, maam."

"Coffee is my specialty.   Anything else, you order at your own risk.   My cooking hasn't killed anyone that I know of.   Maybe a few stumbled off into the sagebrush not to be found 'til spring, but by then I'll have saved enough to retain a lawyer."

His laugh is genuine and holds nothing of his personality back.   She pours his coffee and stands before him, presumably awaiting his menu selection, but her eyes, however discreetly, are checking him out in full detail. He finally decides on a stack of hotcakes.

"Oh, you don't want my hotcakes."

"How 'bout a double order of biscuits and gravy?"

"Not a good choice."

"Bacon and eggs?"

"Wouldn't advise it. I mean, if you want to retain your health and good looks."

"Well, what would you advise?"

"Is there any place else to eat here in town?"

"No."

"How far to the next town?"

"About fourteen miles."

"And I guess you're too hungry to wait 'till six tonight to eat, huh?"

"Well. I…why six P.M.?"

"That's when I get off duty and I like good food too."

His interest, already aroused in this young woman, obviously out of her element here, takes a jump to the next level. The oversized tee shirt and bloused combat pants give her a shapelessness that she probably doesn't deserve. Her raven hair, captured by a long-bibbed baseball cap shades her eyes and makes him want to see her in a more friendly light.

"I suppose I could eat a food bar, come back about six."

"I need at least a half hour to clean-up and change out of these "Lil' Abner" clothes. Pick me up at the motel 'bout six thirty."

"Is there anything I should bring, like a toothbrush?"

"You're not gonna get that lucky, fella."

"One can only hope."

"Hope is what's gettin' you a dinner date. Count your blessing."

"Already doin' that. See you tonight. I'll even wash the pick-up."

"Clean the seats, too."

He swallows the now cold dregs of coffee and leaves.

She watches him drive off and checks the grease stained clock surmounting the "Out of Order" Jukebox. Each booth and table is equipped with a fly swatter, since the one-inch bottom gap on the screen door offers zero deterrent to bugs.

\* \* \* \* \* \*

Showered, shaved and right on time, he's more like a Marlboro Man. She comes from number 13, looking even better than anyone might have imagined. It's an excellent example of serendipity. She's wearing a dark blue skirt that matches her eyes, a simple white blouse and scuffed cowboy boots.

Her long and lustrous shoulder-length hair is down and her coffee-cream complexion sets off her innocent look from fluttering eyelashes. Climbing in beside him, she puts a small shoulder bag on the floor between her feet.

"We've not been formally introduced. I'm Mark Cavendar."

He waits expectantly for her response. It comes, but not as expected. She wiggles the toes of her left foot.

"I wore these corner roach killers cause I figured this would be some line dancing place."

"Do you line dance?"

"Not even on a dare, but I can look the part."

She stares straight ahead, but her peripheral vision catalogues his every move.

14

*Damn, he smells good.  Well, not smelling like horse would have been enough.*

* * * * * *

They finish steaks, fries and a large carafe of generic red wine.  Both refuse desert.  He sits back and assumes a lounging posture.

"So, did I pass the test?"

Her raised eyebrows impressively convey complete incomprehension.

"What do you mean?"

"I've answered all your questions.  The only thing left is checking my fingerprints."

"Well, doesn't someone think highly of himself?  I say it's time to…"

"What, meet your parents?"

"Hardly.  Let's go.  Or do I have to get a buckboard taxi?"

His smile says he's willing to call it a draw.  Leaving cash and a sizable tip, he takes her elbow and escorts her out to his shiny blue truck.  As he holds the passenger door open for her, the metal-to-metal click surprises him, then he realizes that she's handcuffed his right wrist.  She steps out of kicking range and points a snub-nosed .38 at his chest.

"Okay, Hoss, get in."

"Boy, I've had some strange dates, but never been taken captive at gunpoint.  If you just wanted sex, you only needed to ask."

He climbs onto the passenger seat.

"Don't get a swelled head, stud.  I'm very thorough, your finger print I.D. came back before noon.  And I might enjoy wrestling with you, but not while I drive.  So if you make any aggressive move, I'll just tie you up and throw you in back.  You're coming to Vegas with me."

15

"I'll buy a toothbrush and we can get married in Vegas."

"I never marry on a first date."

She cuffs his other hand to the grip-bar on the dash, tightens the seat belt and uses his leather belt to strap his feet together, then slams the door shut on the tail end. He's so well tethered, only his thoughts are free.

"If you're a Vegas cop, read me my rights and take me to a local lock-up."

"You know your rights, Bubba, this is not your first rodeo."

Pulling the truck onto the road and heading for Nevada, she throws gravel in a rooster tail.

"You need extradition papers to take me out of state."

"Oh, cowboy-up. We got word you were in Reno and I flew up to take you into custody."

"That won't float. Witnesses will put me here in Idaho today."

"Only 'til about five. You drove straight to Reno. I found you feeding nickels into the machine, convinced you to accompany me and we sailed down 395. We pulled into Vegas and had a fancy meal before I took you into the house of many slammers."

"Why do you want me? I mean besides the obvious sexual attraction."

At that, she almost puts the F150 into the ditch.

"You know why, but your family connections won't help you this time."

He withholds his response and they ride in silence for an hour before monotony forces her to try the radio. With only morbid C and W songs about being left by Lucille or clones to that effect, she turns it off.

\* \* \* \* \* \*

16

At Jackpot, Nevada she buys a six-pack of bottled water and back on 93 south she keeps below sixty-five. The NHP is very forgiving, but she doesn't want to draw attention to her illicit activity.

In just over two hours they enter Wells, Nevada. She's been up twenty-four hours and starts to nod. She can't make it without sleep. At the first motel, she pays cash and parks two steps from room six. Looking for and seeing no witnesses she drags her shackled captive inside. With the drapes closed and her gun ready, she checks the bathroom and closet. He sprawls on one of the beds, grinning like he's just won the lottery.

"With my hands cuffed I'm severely handicapped. You'll have to take the initiative. Kiss me and put a lot of tongue into it."

"Not gonna happen, slick."

"Damn, I knew I should have brought my toothbrush."

Ignoring his humor, she cuffs him to the metal bed frame and using a small screwdriver she removes the bathroom doorknob.

"Okay, use the bathroom, but have no illusions. If you're ready to die, I'm willing to help."

"Not me, missie. I just wantta rest my baby little head. Safest way is cuff us together, just use the one bed, that way I'm sure to behave. Oh, I sleep in the raw."

"Get into that bathroom."

"You'll have to help me undress."

"My God, do you never quit?"

"Can't win the prize if you don't play the game."

With blue eyes that once seemed warm, now cold, she holds an unblinking stare.

*For a smart guy, he's not the ugliest character I've ever seen.*

He shrugs, shuffles into the bathroom and closes the door halfway.   She's pushing one bed against the front door when she hears the shower running and makes it there in three steps.

"If you think showering in all your clothes will force me to undress you, go ahead.   You'll lie on the floor wet and catch pneumonia for all I care.   I just promised to bring you back.   I never specified "alive.""

He turns off the shower and washes his hands and face.

A small, fast, brown Volvo, following them since Jackpot pulls in.   The driver crosses to the dusty blue pick-up and attaches a small device under the gas tank. The other three men enter the office.   They all enter room 21 across the way.   In the dark room, the curtain is pulled almost shut, but a gap allows two of the men to watch room six.   The others fall immediately asleep atop the two beds.

Laura watches them enter room 21, which never shows a light.   Mark stretches across one bed.

"Don't get too comfy, stud.   We won't be here long."

She dials 911 on a cell phone.

"Police, I've just witnessed a drug buy.   Four men in a brown Volvo just checked into room 21 of the Alpine Motel.   I saw the exchange, but they're getting ready to split.   If you hurry you can still catch them with the goods."

She hangs up, not allowing any questions.   In minutes, three police cars pull quietly to the front of the motel.   As officers approach with guns drawn, she grabs Mark and shuffles him into the dark pick-up.   When the "Open up, Police" is shouted, she pulls the pick-up out the rear of the parking lot.   Back on the highway, she turns on the headlights.  At the Flying J, she gasses up and pays with cash.

"I'm hopelessly turned around.  How ever do I get back onto hiway 80 east?"

Her coy looks and unforgettable profile leave the attendant with a memory he'll be able to pass on.  She heads toward the freeway onramp toward Reno, but uses back streets to reconnect with interstate 93 south.  Once out of town she floors the pedal and is soon the only thing moving on the moonlit road.

\* \* \* \* \* \*

With the arrival of dawn, she pulls into an abandoned dilapidated barn.  Her back trail showing no sign of followers, she takes a length of rope from the junk in the barn and fashions a noose.

Taking the slackness from it, she places it around her captive's neck then pulls the end through the window and rolls it up tight.  With her feet pressed against his knees, he's as secure as if indeed he was dangling from a hangman's noose.

"What the hell's this?"

"I've got to rest and I don't want you wandering off, getting your poor ole self lost."

"Cause you've fallin' for me."

"Whatever rocks your boat, Clyde."

Curling against the far window and her gun in hand, him just a foot away she feels as insecure as sharing the cab with rattlesnakes, but she's taken all the precautions allowed her.

\* \* \* \* \* \*

The warmth of the sun and the sound of goats chewing the rubber bumper guards awaken her.  Wide-awake and staring at her from the same position she left him, he's now grinning.

"You're sure cute when you sleep, even though you drool."

"Do not."

"It's so endearing to learn you have little foibles, after thinking you were perfect."

"What is wrong with you?   I'm taking you to prison and you act like this is your first high school date."

"Yeah, I feel like we're Archie and Veronica and…"

"Cool it."

"You're just upset because I didn't give you my class ring to wear."

\* \* \* \* \* \*

Twilight and the glitter of Las Vegas appear on the horizon.   It's not the fancy meal she'd promised, but a fast food drive-in and because she refuses to unshackle him, she's forced to hand feed him Greasy burritos.

At the Clark County Sheriff's Office, she staggers up the stairs with her prisoner in tow (the rope still around his neck).   She's able to see him taken into custody before collapsing onto a bed and dropping into a deep but troubled sleep in an empty cell.

\* \* \* \* \* \*

Laura wakes to see Mark smiling across at her, sitting comfortably on the opposite bunk.

"What the hell?"

She jumps up and dives for the locked cell door.

"You are so adorable in your sleep.   No lies or convoluted stories, no nonsense about how you can't cook.   Even that little snore, like a small animal cuddled beneath its mama.   And it's precious how your eyes are in REM when you're dreaming about me."

20

"Guard, help! I'm locked in here with a crazy prisoner."

No response to her calls. Mark is holding the cell key. Frantically she feels for her gun, finds it in place. The Sheriff saunters down the aisle, looks through the bars and frowns at her.

"You'd better listen to Deputy Cavendar and agree to his terms. If he brings kidnapping charges against my most promising rookie, I'll be forced to dismiss you with extreme prejudice."

He calmly strolls away, leaving them in the cold, sterile antiseptic-smelling cell. Mark crosses to sit beside her.

"I retired six years ago to raise cutting horses. The Sheriff realized that I bore a remarkable resemblance to Joseph Donofrio, in witness protection for rolling on the family's gaming connections here.
They put out a hit on him; sooner or later they'd have found him. So the Nevada Organized Crime Unit decided to draw the shooters out. They leaked the information about me hiding in Idaho to a smart and ambitious rookie who took the opportunity in her teeth."

"You mean I was bait? Left to twist in the wind?"

"You didn't <u>have</u> to follow the lead, and you were covered by satellite eyes from the time you first headed north. I must say they had no clue of your resourcefulness. You could teach Guantanamo how to take a prisoner illegally, torture him, and abuse his civil rights. Unfortunately, if I tell, you'll be thrown to the wolves."

"And…if you <u>don't</u> tell?"

"Well, you might convince me that my memory was foggy and unreliable."

"And just when and how would I do this?"

"Over dinner at Caesars.' By the way, my intended killers, caught with a dozen illegal weapons and collected through your call, are all in custody and, facing life times three. They've all rolled. The entire family is behind bars and under federal indictment."

*Damn, for a good lookin' dude, he's not the dumbest I've ever come across.*

"So, this…dinner. I suppose you'd want to bring your toothbrush along?"

"Well, hope doth spring eternal."

He pulls her tight and concentrating on the kiss, he lets her slip the cell keys from his fingers.

#

How much money would you have if you had one (only one) example of each denomination of coin and paper currency ever issued by the United States? Answer somewhere in a later edition.

#

# 2-SOUTHERN COMFORT

## *CEDAR GROVE-NORTH CAROLINA, AUGUST*

Matt, thirty something, short brown curly hair, clean casual clothes sits among smelly, nervous men and aging, underdressed, over-cosmetized women. Through the high, narrow, open windows, the song of robins, rustling oak leaves, saltwater-tasting air, and other elements of freedom assail him. The generic courtroom clock hands seem fixed at 3:27. His attention is brought sharply back to the day's event by the harsh rap of a gavel. The brass nameplate informs all that District Court Judge Wilma C. Osborne presides.

Wilma, twenty-nine, single, slight, looking even more so in the smallest black robe the county provides, calls the court to attention. "Next case."

The sheriff steps to the oak barrier that separates the haves from the have-nots. "Vagrancy, withholding evidence and impeding a lawful investigation, your honor."

The judge scans a bunch of papers and looks down at Matt. "I've read the arrest report. What have you to say for yourself, young man?"

Matt moves to the open space before the judge's high bench. His demeanor shows nothing of the penitent.

"Oh, after two and a half hours of incarceration I finally get to tell my story?" He grins lopsidedly and looks up into the unblinking eyes of the woman who holds his immediate future in her hand. Turning, he speaks more directly to the audience. "I was arrested and held incommunicado, not even told the charge."

The sheriff jumps to his feet. "Judge, we was lookin' for the guy burglarized the general store out past the interstate when we caught this guy just outside the town limits. I asked for his I.D. and he give me static. Even refused to supply his name."

Matt shakes his head and frowns. "Justice in a small town for someone without clout."

Judge Osborne frowns. "Young man, speak only to the counts with which you're charged."

"Well, I was walking down a country road, bothering no one when I was accosted by your storm-troopers."

"What were you doing in our county? What is your business?"

"My own. I was minding it at the time."

"You refused to assist the officers by showing them identification.    You claimed you have no driver's license."

"I was walking, didn't know I needed a license for that in your county."

"What is your name, sir?"

"You can call me John."

"Is that your real name?"

"It's a good old Anglo-Saxon name, a biblical name, the name of kings, a name to be proud of.   Why should I be ashamed of it?"

"I didn't suggest you should be ashamed of it. I…look, you refused to answer any of the sheriff's questions and I'd like to know why."

"He didn't ask, he demanded.   I told him I'd done nothing illegal.   It wasn't good enough for him."

"Sheriff, in the investigation of a crime, did you ask the defendant to identify himself?   Did he refuse?   Did he fail to provide proper identification?"

"Objection, leading the witness."

"You can't object; you're the defendant, not a lawyer."

"You don't know that."

"Are you a member of the North Carolina bar?"

"No, but doesn't there have to be probable cause to question a citizen, or did I sleep twenty years and wake-up in the middle of the Third Reich?"

"Sheriff?"

"Judge, twenty cows been rustled outta Smith's Bog a'ready this month.   This guy was suspicious, jest amblin' along like he had no care in the world."

"I had none, until I walked into your tourist trap. Did I have any ruminants in my possession, or any high tech implements of the rustler's trade on me?"

"Huh?"

"Rope, running iron, cattle truck, a drooling gang of cutthroats waiting to carry away the purloined cud-chewers into the land of immoral greed?"

"Uh, well no, but…"

"Did I run, like the cunning villain you expected?"

"No, that's where you made your first mistake. Your honor, he had a whole pocket full of cash.   Like he was ready to pay off his gang."

"And do what, thank them and wish them on their merry way, thence to take charge of these fictitious bovine and lead them to my hide-out?   Naturally I'd feed them from the hundred pounds of oats that filled my pockets.   Or was I to graze them slowly as I worked my way, unhampered to…, just where was I to take them?"

"Well…maybe you was wantin' to buy drugs."

"Oh, are there drug dealers hiding between the rows of tobacco in every field I passed?   I expect my cash will be returned as soon as my attorney arrives.   I will otherwise need to add theft to my lawsuit against this town, county and state for illegal detention."

The judge's gavel strikes a reverberating note. "The initial charge was noncompliance with a request from a law officer in the engagement of his duties.   I am striking that and all subsequent charges.   You cannot sue for a non-action.   Your property will be returned and you are free to go.   Sheriff, have one of your deputies see to it."

"I can do it myse…"

"No, one of your newest deputies.   Now."

Matt makes no move to leave.   "I can still sue for false arrest."

"There's no reason to believe that you would win."

"But if I sue for one dollar and win, what would your political backers think?   Would I sue here in this court, in front of you?"

"You will have no evidence to put forward.  I am expunging the arrest record and I hope you reconsider such a brash act.  Such a case could be tied up in the system for years and cost you a small fortune just to win a moral victory."

"Sometimes a moral victory is all a man has, all that survives him.  Maintaining our morals is what allows us to rise above the beasts of the fields.  But I might reconsider if I get an apology from the sheriff."

The lawman's face turns a bright red, matching his neck.

Without benefit of electrical impulse from his brain, his hand moves toward the six-shooter at his hip.  "I'm not gonna'…"

"Sheriff, you will apologize.  Here and now."

The offensive words scramble within his throat, fighting to stay put.  "I…, well, I'm right sorry if you was inconvenienced, just cause you was suspicious and we…"

"Sheriff, I want a real apology or I'll find you in contempt of court."

"What's that mean?"

Matt, showing glee says,  "Means you'll spend time in your own lock-up.  Take my cell, I'm through with it."

"I'll answer in my own court, thank you.  It means, sheriff, that you'll spend time in your own lock-up."

"You can't do that to me."

"I beg your pardon?"

"I'm not gonna…Well, uh, oh, I'm real sorry 'bout the whole thing.  There, that do it?"

Matt looks up into the face of the jurist and turns on a dazzling smile.  "Why, how could I resist such a gracious and heartfelt performance?  I accept."

"Good, you're free to go.  Court is adjourned.  Sheriff, my office, now, and leave your weapon with my bailiff."

The courtroom empties. Matt strolls out into the soft, warm, magnolia-scented Carolina afternoon. The buzz of dragonflies, the sounds of playing children and the smell of barbeque smoke drift lazily on the light breeze. Twenty minutes later, Wilma leaves the courthouse. In dark, tailored, ultra conservative clothes and huge dark glasses, she hurries toward a no-nonsense, dark-blue Chevy Nova.

Her chestnut hair, down and curled outward from her neck, makes her look ten years younger, but no less wanting for something she doesn't yet recognize.

Matt, atop a fire hydrant in front of her marked parking space watches her every move. He smiles at her involuntary hesitation when she finally sees him. With her key in the lock, she is ready to jerk open the car door. "I've considered your plea. I'll not sue on the condition that you have dinner with me."

"You must be joking. I couldn't possibly be seen with a criminal element."

"I thought I was released without prejudice."

"How do you know that legal term?"

"Not important. To sue, or not to sue, your call."

"I...well, I guess it couldn't hurt to show a damn Yankee some true southern hospitality. There's a great seafood restaurant not far. We'll take my car, that is, if you don't have religious convictions against motor vehicles."

"Oh, no ma'am. I once rode in a Pierce Arrow Cabriolet, but I wouldn't want to do it again. Gracious, it near took my very breath away at past twenty miles an hour. Land sakes, 'taint natural for man to travel at that speed."

"Okay, wipe your feet and get in." In such close proximity she seems to recognize the light scent of Old Spice, unexpected from someone tramping the hot, dusty back roads.    It's mildly discomforting and her driving shows it.

They park beneath a moss-hung cypress that might be a thousand years old.    Climbing the springy gangplank, they enter a restaurant converted from an ocean-going barge.

A large black woman waddles over to them, takes Wilma's hands and leads them to an oilcloth-covered table between pecky-cedar columns that support a glass roof not quite covering the span.    The open edges give complete ventilation and rainwater is drained through the many floor grates spaced for those frequent events.

Matt grins up at their hostess.    "We'll start with shrimp cocktails and vodka martinis and would you chill a bottle of your best champagne for the main course?" The smile that splits her face reflects the candlelight from her front gold tooth like spotlights off a disco-ball.

"Water for me and coffee with the main course, thank you, Martha."

"Oh, let yoself go, girl; you off the clock now and I can't member last time you brung a man here.    And never one so yummy.    Umm, umm, umm.    He could put his shoes 'neath my bed anytime."

Wilma frowns and counters,    "Just the water, thank you."    Martha is gone before a retort can be formed, but her hearty laugh causes vibrations that rattle the glassware.

"You don't drink vodka?    My saintly mother told me to never trust a gin drinker."

"I don't drink vodka or gin.    New Years Eve I'll have one glass of champagne.    Now if you'll excuse me, I'll visit the powder room."    While she's gone, he corners Martha and whispers his idea into her ear.    Her nod and grin indicate that a plan B won't be needed.

Over the shrimp cocktails, Matt keeps the conversation about Wilma. "So how'd you decide to become a judge, some need to express your latent power over lawbreakers? Wanting to see criminals do hard time for jaywalking, the death row for insulting a cop?"

She smiles and demurs in silence. The main course (crab-stuffed eggplant for her and broiled swordfish for him) arrives.

He digs in like a man fresh from Devil's Island. "Doing hard time in the Big House gives a man an appetite."

She has barely begun her entrée when noisemakers fill the air. Martha throws paper streamers into the air, wishes everybody a Happy New Year and fills their two glasses with champagne.

Wilma, not lost on the ploy says to Matt, "It's the middle of May and I'm not drinking just because YOU say its New Years."

But the crowd around them, caught-up in the story, chant "toast, toast, toast." And when she finally gives in and drains her glass in one swallow, he's holding a sprig of mistletoe over her head.

"Happy New Year, darling." His kiss is tender and sweet.

Her mind races.

*No, wait. The sweet is from the champagne, and he's refilling my glass and dipping a strawberry into it, holding it for me to take.*

She takes.

*This is crazy; I'm not some little bimbo, falling for the slick line of a handsome stranger.*

She wills herself to concentrate on food, good food, her favorite food in her favorite restaurant.

"I've never been in this area, are there books on the history and sights?"

"Yes, I have…I mean the library has an interesting selection." She finishes the meal not looking up from her plate.

*No I would not care for desert. I just want to get out of here while I still have some semblance of my dignity left.*

While paying the bill, he takes the car keys from her hand and says, "I'd better drive, you did have that sip of champagne."

Thankfully, in the cool shadows from the huge pyracantha bush, he leads her to the car, holds open the passenger door.

She balks. "Now, see here, I'm not drunk and…" It's impossible for her not to observe the phenomenon of the moon, just breaking the Atlantic horizon creating a scene from the juiciest, most romantic movie you've ever seen. He fumbles with the ignition, letting the ambiance affect her. If anything can, this will.

"Do you want to tell me where you live or should I just drive around until someplace looks familiar?"

## *1212 Oak Harbor Circle-Evening*

He unlocks the apartment door and she quickly slips in, holding her hand out for the keys, keeping the door at a narrow angle, not allowing him to push past her. "Contrary to what you may believe, I was not about to force myself upon you, however…" He aims a light kiss on her slightly open lips. "I thought you might offer a nightcap. You know, the Olde Southern Hospitality thing." A moment's hesitation is her downfall. Cautious to make no physical contact that she might misinterpret, he slides past her into the apartment. "You have a lovely place with a marvelous view."

"I don't have any liquor so it'll be coffee or water and then you're gone."

He pulls the almost full bottle of champagne from behind his back. "Got that covered." He opens the French doors leading onto a fire escape. "Shall we have our drinks on the terrace?"

"Drink, your drink, your <u>one</u> drink." His crestfallen expression is that of a small boy whose football has just been crushed by an eighteen-wheeler. She stiffens her back, but she heads into the kitchenette, returning with two small sherbet glasses. He's already shaken out two canvas director's chairs on the fire-escape/terrace.

\* \* \* \* \* \*

Wilma awakens at the sound of a tomcat prowling the back alley. The first flash of terror hits her. In the dark she reaches across the queen-size bed and feels only cold sheets. She calms, realizing that it's all been a dream (scratch that, a nightmare). As her pulse returns to normal, she gets up to take an aspirin. In the thin light of predawn she notices the unlocked French doors. Only when her hand reaches for the knob does she see the empty champagne bottle and two glasses, one lipstick marked. Shaky knees take her back to the bedroom, but knowing she'll be unable to sleep, she runs a shower. Feeling once again in control after shower, shampoo, fresh make-up and the new summer dress she'd been saving for the Founder's Day picnic she returns to the bedroom. Being one to make the bed before it gets cold, she can't miss the note, there on the second pillow. She slips it into her purse. Her keys are on the end table, not hanging on the hallway rack where she always keeps them.

The first misdemeanor cases are easily dispatched and the next defendant is a no show.

She can break for lunch, but with two hours free time she'd never be able to avoid thinking. She calls a fifteen-minute recess and steps into her chambers. Only when alone, with not enough time to get nervous no matter what it says, she opens the note.

*Dear Claire, (from your car registration) I prefer to remember our connection as special. I haven't the words to tell you how much last night meant to me, and I hope meant to you.*

*My fingerprints will be on the bottle and I'll understand if you feel the need to have me traced. I hope you don't, you wouldn't learn anything negative, but I'll explain fully when I return.*

*Matt (A.K.A., John)*

A knock at the door and the bailiff announces, "Judge, court's ready if you are?"

She shoves the note in her pocket and re-enters the courtroom. Her step is hesitant.

## CEDAR GROVE, NORTH CAROLINA, NOVEMBER

Judge Wilma C. Osborne has finally (almost) (maybe) forgotten Matt when the bailiff draws her attention to an Idaho Journal story picked up on The American Bar's website. Matt is pictured and identified as Matthew Stuart.

"The district attorney's influence peddling case against Idaho State Senator Jonathan Stuart has been withdrawn as a result of new evidence. The original charge stated that Jonathan solicited money from the elusive J.D. Allmot to sway the vote on sending fifty-five thousand tons of frozen French fries to China through the Allmot Wholesale Food Corporation. Stuart's defense attorney, his brother Matt, ferreted Allmot from hiding in rural North Carolina. Allmot has admitted he was under duress to fulfill his obligation under a contract with unnamed underworld figures and hoped to deflect attention by implicating Jonathan. Matthew Stuart's single-handed ability to find Allmot and bring him to indictment has started a domino effect, exposing a proposed international trade that would have brought twenty tons of heroin into the United States."

One retirement home in Boise has a waiting list
while others operate at less than capacity.  Our
investigation shows their Bloody Mary brunch, three
martini lunch, mid-afternoon Irish Coffee and
evening Mai Tai buffet may have some small effect
on the smiles of those residents interviewed.

#

# 3-ANSWERING THE CALL OF DUTY

The Sheriff holds the rope loosely in one hand, his
head hangs low, but thankfully the ancient live-oak tree
keeps his face in shadow.   No one sees the tears that
come unbidden to the eyes in his parchment-textured face.
Removing his sweat-stained Stetson, he shakes his head,
casting aside the evidence of his salt-ladened anguish.
The action of what he is about to do, must do, is an
incriminating accusation of his total failure as a human
being.

A second man spurs his horse to bring him
alongside the Sheriff.   "Gotta be done, Hank, but it don't
gotta be you."

Without reply the Sheriff turns to face the twenty
mounted deputies.   Sunlight reflects off the star on his
chest and blazes like the finger of an accusing deity.   The
sinews of his flexed arm tighten as he swings the rope in
an increasing rhythm until he lets go and it flies from his
callused hand.    Twenty feet above, it loops over a
horizontal branch and allows the hangman's noose to
swing innocently in the light south Texas breeze.

A young man, his hands tied behind his back, is led from
the center of the posse and positioned under the oak.   His
horse is lathered, its' sides streaked with angry rowel

34

gashes, it's mouth dripping blood from the bit that has sawed it raw.

From the waiting posse, "You know it don't hafta end thisaway, Hank. You could just go on back to town and let us handle this."

The boy looks down at the Sheriff playing out the rope until it hangs to the boy's chest. One deputy holds the boy's horse; another reaches up, flips the boy's hat off and slips the noose around his neck. The horse flinches at movement from a nearby iguana. Calmed by soft talk from the man holding the reins, the horse stands hipshot as the man tightens and adjusts the rope across the boy's left ear and under his chin. A third deputy separates from the group, dismounts and ties the loose end of the rope around the trunk of the oak. The Sheriff, refusing to look up, pulls the vest across his chest, covering the star, as if to deny the sign of his office and refuse his duty, but the whip in his hand is ready. Fear and humiliation show in every part of the boy's slumped posture.

Turning as best he can, he speaks to the Sheriff. "I'm sorry, pa. I never meant no harm. It was ony a couple cayuses. I was gonna sellum 'cross the border. I never thought…"

"Prepare to meet yor maker, boy."

At the last second, a deputy pushes him away and a wicked blow from his open hand across the horse's flank sends it, wide eyed, across the dusty prairie. The squeak of the stretched rope and the sweet call of doves on the branches above the swinging body are the only sounds to be heard as the posse turns quietly for home.

Yes, it's true the zoning law says you COULD cut off the top of your unused septic tank to make it into a swimming pool, but I must say, it's really not advisable.

#

# 4-A SISTER'S LOVE

A million stars blink a welcome to lovers. Hand in hand they leave the party and head into the moonlit desert. Ten miles away, Las Vegas lights the horizon and competes with nature for title of best lighting effect. It's the romantic setting that movie directors envision. Julius knew he would get lucky tonight. The soft breeze on their faces tells them they're heading west into the foothills, but the darkness and the loose sand hides all other sign and leaves no trace of their passage.

She's young, too young to know what she's doing, but she'll learn; he'll teach her. It's not the first time he's had a virgin in his sights and he's a credible marksman.

He pulls her to him and kisses her. He's willing to stop and drop, take her right here, in the sand.

"Not yet." She breathes huskily in his ear. "After I show you what's out here."

He'd only half believed her about this Silver mine her old man had quit just after his stroke. The idea that anyone would have a claim so well hidden that it was never found is hard to believe. Metal detector-carrying desert rats comb this whole area for that very thing. But, what the hell, he had no reason not to look. There's always the chance it's true.

She draws him on. How far they've come, he hasn't a clue, but then she stops and jerks away a dirt-covered tarp and sure enough, there it is, the opening to an abandoned mine. There's no light out here and he hadn't believed her enough to bring a flashlight, but she'd said there were acetylene lamps just to the left, along the shelf, so he shuffles his feet along carefully, an inch or two at a time. It goes slowly at first, then,

His scream is heard by her, a few lizards, insects, maybe a mouse or two, but none others. The old saw about "does a tree falling in the forest make any sound if there's no one to hear," a good example here.

She'd planned it well. The fall has obviously broken one or both his legs.

She leans into the dark abyss and calls down to him. "Make all the noise you want. It will attract rattlesnakes even sooner. You don't remember, but a year ago to the day, you brought my sister out to one of these Raves. You got her hooked on Ecstasy and heroin, raped her and left her alone out here. When she learned she was pregnant and hooked on drugs, she committed suicide. The police said there was nothing they could do. I was just fifteen. The District Attorney wouldn't even investigate. Somebody had to do something and my parents weren't up to it."

From her pocket, she takes out two dried rattles, souvenirs available from many desert roadside stands and with finality she throws them into the hole. The cooing of the desert breeze drowns his terrified screams as he hears the rattles. Ella calmly retraces her path to the waiting car, leaving him to the fast, merciful death of heart attack or more slowly, the hungry creatures of the night.

#

Why does the opening logo of a picture show the studio's name wrapped around the <u>Earth</u> when they call themselves "<u>Universal</u> Studio?"

#

## 5-COLD

*Where did I put my glasses? Somebody's always moving my stuff. Let's see, in the drawer, watch, papers, gold ring, inscribed...don't need glasses to read...J.B. With all my love. M.B. Oh, God, why didn't I tell you more often how much you meant to me?...sh, too loud. If you're too loud they'll be in and...pills, two, no, three. You'd think it would destroy their schedule if they had to...oh; here they are under the pillow. Now, two? No, three. There, ugh, dry without water. Margaret, I loved you so much and we had so little time together. Apart all I have are memories. There're great, but not enough.*

*That summer in Venice with the Berlitz dictionary, we thought we were ordering dinner and the waiter said we'd asked for a red boat with goat cheese. And Athens, where you couldn't get enough of the brown figs so you hid some in your luggage and they fermented in the heat and we laughed and laughed and then... Three more, ugh.*

*Then the blue Capri sky that matched your eyes. The clean smell of the air at Jackson Hole when they closed the hiking trails to the public and we snuck under the rope and climbed halfway to heaven. The freezing water of the Snake River where you dared me to skinny-dip. Your cool fingertips on my brow that summer atop a bare, Chilean cliff as we waited for the afternoon thermals.*

38

*They said we were too old to take up hang-gliding, said we should go home and leave it to the kids.   Thought we were too old to make love, too.   That's how much they knew.   Remember that sunset on the balcony overlooking the Serengeti?*

*Why didn't they let me bring that bottle of Napoleon brandy we started in Paris and never got to finish? Three, no, empty.   Where's that other bottle?   Here, under the mattress…three?   No, all at once.   Now they're all gone.*

*Cold, so cold, why don't they tell you it's so cold…you'd think they'd give me another blanket if they only knew how cold it is.   Oh, hell, let them find out when their time comes.   Is it cold there, Margaret?   Or does it ever warm up?  So cold.  I'm coming, Margaret.  I'm…*

"Mr. Bedart?   Mr. Bedart, it's time for your medication, Mr. Bedart?  Mr.…..Bedart?"

#

Take heart all you would-be authors:  Walt
Whitman sold only three-dozen copies of his
first edition of "Leaves of Grass."

#

# 6-DONALD DUMONT, PRIVATE EYE

Picture a warm sultry Friday night, the kind that San Francisco is famous for having so few of.   The Kress' three-dollar curtains rustled at the open window of my seventh floor office of the Monadnock Building.     I frowned at the empty White Horse bottle and wondered how I'd managed to neglect replenishing such an important office staple.   The fog-heavy air tasted salty and forced me to consider the double Scotch I was missing to make it perfect.   I considered fighting the three-deep stockbrokers and bankers who crowd the after-work bars on Sutter Street.

I hadn't decided, when my outer office door opened and a pair of million dollar legs walked in. They were attached to a tall, slender blonde with just the right combination of smile and pout. She could talk, too, although I know you're thinking that probably spoiled it. Well, I hadn't had a case in over a week and the rent was due. Sure, I could pony up the thirty-seven fifty from my inheritance, but first I'd have to find some rich couple to adopt me.

"Mr. Dumont? My cousin Gladys in Santa Rosa said you're the best private detective in Frisco."

"She's right. Now why's a swell dame like you need a gumshoe?"

She coiled herself onto the hard uncomfortable oak chair I keep so visitors won't stay long.

"My husband Karl made me leave our home in Lewiston, Idaho. He was afraid of something, but he wouldn't tell me what. It may be bank business. We own the only one in town.
I was to check into the Fairmont, do some shopping, see some plays at the Curran, maybe take in a vaudeville or two at the Golden Gate Theater."

"And what exactly do you want me to do, Mrs.?"

"Engle, Judith Engle. I want you to fix whatever my husband is afraid of."

"That's all? You don't want me to ride Seabiscuit in the Kentucky Derby while riding backwards and playing Amazing Grace on bagpipes?"

"I realize it sounds like a lot. That's why I need the best shamus in town."

"Well, I'll go look around, it could take a couple o' weeks and I can't promise anything until I know more."

"That sounds reasonable. This envelope has our home address, a photo of my husband and a retainer of five thousand. I hope that's enough."

"That'll do just fine. I'll get started on it tonight, contact you at the Fairmont when I have news."

"Oh, here's the key to my new LaSalle, it's parked at the Spokane airport."

As soon as she left I left her check for my secretary to deposit. Southern Pacific made my sleeper reservation on the Coast Starlight. I had just enough time to pick up traveling necessities at the Owl drug store (plus a canvas travel bag for the two pints of White Horse). A Yellow Cab got me to Third and Townsend in time to grab a cardboard carton of coffee and a couple of donuts before boarding the shuttle bus to the Oakland train depot.

\* \* \* \* \* \*

The train clack-clacked it's way north with enough daylight to see the frontage roads and the week-end traffic of farm trucks and kids in their sooped-up flivvers. With the dining car filling with families and salesmen anxious to talk, I chose the club car and dined on hot-roasted peanuts, Schlitz beer and soft piano music (mostly Gershwin).

*Perfect time and place to ask myself difficult questions like did I really want to find her husband...alive. The thought of her, a new car and wads of dough fought with keeping me on the right side of respectability.*

\* \* \* \* \* \*

Portland at dawn, not enough time for ham and shirred eggs aboard. I was deposited along with yokels carrying cardboard suitcases and rope-tied burlap bundles.

*Okies come to the land of the setting sun where magic crops needed no water and cut themselves into piles ready to be loaded aboard wagons pulled by sensitive and caring mules.*

I transferred to the Great Northern's two car "Express" to Spokane and thought about the possibilities.

*He skipped out on with bank funds, had gambling debts, was running from the mob, he was messin' with somebody-else' tail. With what he had at home, he'd have been crazy, but I liked that scenario best.*

\* \* \* \* \* \*

Spokane, and a man so thin he'd probably crumble before I reached his (black, of all colors) Model T taxi and put-putted me out to the Spokane airport.
I woke up the clerk at the only counter at this dirt strip. He looked like he wasn't older than a hundred and six and he'd died thirty years ago only nobody'd told him. With several maps and some coffee that'd probably been brewed during FDR's first inaugural address, I picked up her car and headed east.

Crossing into Idaho the pace immediately slowed by about twenty years. I pulled into the first fishing camp. There's probably no bad time or place to fish in Idaho and I was lucky it wasn't crowded, serious anglers choosing much harder to get to places.

*Sheer obstinacy I expect.*

From what I'd heard folks here welcome strangers even at suppertime. But my probing could wait until morning. I checked into a three dollar a night boarding house, and being basically a steak and potato guy, I expected no elegant fare in Hicksville, but was pleasantly surprised. That days' catch of trout was better than any I'd had at four-star San Francisco restaurants. And YES baked potatoes like you could only get from this state.

I'm used to sitting cramped in my '32 coupe for long stretches on stakeouts so I'm not fussy about physical comforts and these rustic surroundings were fine.

*Somehow I pictured Judith...ah...Mrs. Engle in a more elegant setting.   Well, I'll see when I meet Karl on his own turf.*

\* \* \* \* \* \*

After an amazing breakfast of quail egg soufflé, salmon croquettes, coffee and hot biscuits with home made clover honey I was ready to leave.

*More ready to stay.   I can see now why people move up to a place like this, but I need to get on the road.*

Shaded sections of the narrow, twisting road retained snow and I made poor time.   Finally reaching Lewiston in early afternoon I started my search on the poorly marked trails.   I stopped at a coffee shop and bait stand.   The woman in charge--proprietor by the way she smiled at me even before I pushed open the screen door. She was built like Ma. Kettle.

"Can I get a cup o' joe and ask a question?"

"Coffee's a dime, answers are free, stranger."

She turned to the big urn and poured me a cup of steaming, black, surpy coffee.

"Do you know a couple named Engle?"

Her back stiffened and although she recovered before turning to face me, it was a better answer than any her lips would give me.

"Heard tell they got a place some'ers about, but don't recollect ever meetin'um in person, like.   Gettja anything ta go with the coffee, mister?"

"Not unless you can direct me to...Dolly Varden Lane?"

"Fraid not."

43

*Jaws clenched and words forced between tightened teeth.*

Back in the car, I pulled away slowly enough to catch her holding back the chintz curtain to watch me leave.  It took an hour to find the place.

*No answer to bell or knocking; dark inside.*

At a small window out of view from the road, I slipped the thin blade of my pocketknife between the double-hung window lock, I was inside in seconds, listening for any sounds of life.

*Nothing but doves cooing on the porch and deer decimating the garden of double-ruffled petunias.*

*Huge open rustic living room, decorated with Indian rugs and large, overstuffed leather couches and chairs, hardly anywhere a woman's touch.  Cut-glass vases, filled with lilies, irises and daffodils (all drooping,) geometrically arranged books; Hemingway, Vardis Fisher, Mari Sandoz, Mary Austin, artwork of Ansel Adams, Remington & Russell.  Master bedroom, bed not made sheets cold, bathroom a mess, bath towel on the floor, long blonde hair in the sink, toothpaste tube squeezed in middle, hand towel used to wipe dust from shoes; Kitchen, milk not spoiled, eggs, butter, canned peaches, sardines all at room temperature.*

*Two to three days, not more.*

I climbed back out the window and closed it after me.  A mile away middle-aged couple rocking on the front porch of a cabin.  He smoked a burl-wood pipe as she de-silked corn.  With hummingbirds clustered at feeders hung from the eves.  I could swear I was looking at full scale Hummel Figures.  I left the car door open and walked to the rough-hewn balustrade.

"Excuse the interruption, but I was to meet a Mr. Engel at his address, but there doesn't seem to be any sign of him.  Do you happen to know if he's in town?"

*Same body language as at the bait store.*

"We know nothing about him or his kind, don't care to."

I left them to their isolationism and tried further down the same road. A man about thirty, torn undershirt and muscular build scraping the bottom of an old worm-eaten wooden rowboat.

*He'll be at that long after the season is over.    More work than it's worth.*

*Sears sells new ones for a hundred forty-nine bucks, but I guess up here that's three month's wages.*

"Say, I was looking to get in a little time on the water myself. Guy in town said a fella name of Engle could show me the best spot to throw a line in, but I can't find his place."

He looked me over like I'd come to take his thirteen-year old daughter to a local roadhouse.

"It's up the road a piece.    Got a whole yard fulla petunias his wife protects like they was Fort Knox. But…I never heerd of him fishin, didn't know he even had a pole, much less a boat."

"What kinda guy is he?    You know him well?"

"Just ta wave at or talk bout weather down to the general store."

*He never misses his boat scraping by even half-a-beat.*

"Okay, say could I get a sandwich and a brew at that general store?"

"Sure, if ya want a sandwich been sittin' in the case for close on a week.    Better try the "Hook-In-Mouth." It's right on the main drag."

*Not smart to ask more.    Fish and fishing is the thing to do, talk or think about.*

The general store was only ten yards from the Hook-In-Mouth.    I tried it first.

45

The old guy slouched over the counter had the watery eyes (even showing the haw) and droopy jowls of a bloodhound. His voice, even at a low conversational volume vibrated cans on the shelves. I bought a newspaper, two packs of Lucky Strikes, threw a quarter on the counter and watched for his reaction, as he was busy opening a tin cash-box.

"I'm told trout can smell cigarette smoke a long way off. I'm going out with Mr. Engel. Do you know if he smokes while he's fishing?"

He threw my change onto the counter and although not raising his voice his words made his point as clear as if he'd carved it in the plank counter with a Bowie knife.

"Take your stuff and get out. You don't wanna ever come in my store again."

Standing, he towered above me by almost a foot. The rolls of fat and flabby arms didn't fool me. I could probably take him, but it wouldn't be fun.

Next door, the checkered tablecloth and beer bottle with weeping candle tried vainly to give the place a homey feel, but the twenty-something honey-blonde with dimples she could hide dimes in made it work. I was her only customer and I didn't see any short-order cook.

"Can I get a couple of grilled cheese sandwiches and a cold brew? Bring a beer for yourself, yours is the first friendly face I've seen so far."

She brought my order, included coffee for herself and curled herself into an uncomfortable-looking chair.

*Comparing the picture of my office and Judith gracefully poured into the guest chair, this is a girl, Judith is a woman.*

She clinked her sugar spoon on her cup bringing me back to earth.

"I said, if you're looking for Mr. Engle, you should talk to my husband. He runs this Inn. He's out right now, but he'll be back bit later."

*Would that be a friendly contact or another Engle hater?*

"Thanks, I'll amble around town, come back in an hour."

A couple of blocks away an unpainted building housed the public library, local museum and phone company. I hit the library first.

\* \* \* \* \* \*

It had been a very productive afternoon. I wasn't sure I was any closer to finding Karl, but I think I knew why he was missing. Back at the Inn, a well built man of about thirty, smiled, introduced himself as Stephen Bock, owner.

"I'm looking for Mr. Engel, I was told you two were friends."

"In fact, I just spoke to him by phone. If you'll follow me into my office you can call him yourself."

Freedom and safety were scant minutes behind me. Unfortunately, I went forward.

\* \* \* \* \* \*

The blow behind the ear put me out and when I came to, I was tied into a chair and eight men with murderous looks surrounded me. One of the two leveling pistols at my head was the helpful Inn Keeper. I'd never seen the others, but except for the uniformed Sheriff, I knew who they were. By name and occupation. Nine men, banker, teacher, printer, lawyer, doctor, minister, innkeeper, sheriff, trail-guide. The banker was missing, but all the others had a similar ethnic look.

"Where is she?"

47

"Who?"

The first kick to my side was enough to break a couple of ribs. The pain of inhaling told me that much without need of an X-ray.

"You know who, Mrs. Engle."

The second kick took me high on the face, blackened my eye and sliced a flap of skin that fell like an open transom onto my cheek.

"Now the best doctors will never repair that well enough to make me the matinee idol I've always been."

The sheriff advanced on me this time, intent on doing some real damage.

"Smart guy, huh?"

I held myself loose to roll with the punch, but it didn't help much, just kept me from blacking out.

*Maybe not such a good idea after all.*

Trying not to show discomfort, I shook my head and confronted my attackers.

"I figure you were probably landed by German sub in '34, somewhere north of Vancouver. You made your way across country, heading east. Probably split up soon after crossing into northern Idaho."

"Where would you get such a preposterous idea?"

"When I learned you'd all been here less than three years, I contacted the R.C.M.P. The tracks showed where a hay truck had gone off the road. The farmer was killed and left beside the road, his truck missing. The Mounties assumed it was a simple car theft gone bad when the truck was found five hundred mile north of here."

"What's that to do with us?"

"They didn't make the connection, because the jacketed bullet that killed the farmer was a .35 caliber. They figured some kind of .38. But a hundred-ten grains is light for revolvers, which use cheap lead bullets; semi-autos <u>need</u> jackets to feed properly.   That pretty much describes one like that 9-millimeter Luger you're pointing at me.   You were looking for someplace to re-emerge where you'd fit in.

I'm guessing Engle found this place and set up a small bank to introduce each of you as entrepreneurs looking to settle in a small community."

"You couldn't know that, it's some fantastic fiction you've invented."

"No, you planned well, but you weren't very original, Engle, Schmidt, Wagner, Bock, etc., all Americanized Germanic names.   Were you to stay low, build a spy network or were you to sabotage war plants in the event we came into your war?"

They looked at each other, shrugged.

"Nothing so dramatic.   We were to cultivate your isolationist policy.   If successful here others would be sent."

"You must have pushed too hard, you Germans have a habit of doing that.   When you stirred up animosity among the locals, why didn't you just pick up your marbles and go home?"

"We'd built a good life and decided to expand the original concept.   It's too late to do much immediate good for the Fatherland, but we can watch the Third Reich grow here."

"How, by interbreeding with the local frauleins and creating a race of Supermen?   That's not a short term plan."

"Granted, but in two generations we can make this whole country see the beauty of "Strength through Joy."

"You're telling me all this because you've nothing to lose.   You krauts are going to kill me anyway, but I've left an indelible trail.   There're eight of you here so you've already done away with Engle, and you obviously think he told his wife something he shouldn't have. He didn't."

"We'll decide that for ourselves, but to satisfy your curiosity, we had to eliminate Engle. He was a weak link, gone soft with this easy American living."

"Why are you telling him that, Wagner?"

"What's the difference, Klaus? He knows we can't let him live."

"He's a private investigator from San Francisco. She must have hired him. We'll go there, wait in his office until she shows up."

"Won't do you any good. I called her, told her to stay out of touch and notify the F.B.I."

"He's bluffing. Kurt, go see Stella at the phone company, find out if he placed any long distance calls to San Francisco."

"See, smart boy, in a minute we'll know and it will be just as if you never existed."

"Oh I exist. We existed long before there was a Germany and we'll be here when it's just another satellite of Russia."

"What do you mean before…?"

"Your ancestors were living in skin tents and throwing spears at anything you could eat raw 'cause you hadn't found fire while my people were making deserts bloom. I anglicized my name just like you, but by accident. The prior tenant of my office was Donald Dumont–Psychiatrist. The sign painter was short on gold paint so I kept the name and just had him change the Psychiatrist to Private Eye. My real name is Danny Diamond."

"I knew it. He's a Jew Bastard."

That kick mercifully put me out. I never heard the shot or felt the hundred-ten grain slug that sent me to join Father Abraham, Isaiah and King David.

The Spokane Daily Register the next day carried the following story:

"Sheriff Eberhardt of Lewiston, Idaho has solved a murder/suicide case. Karl Engle's body, found below a cliff is classified as death with unusual circumstances. He had a new fishing pole, but no flies and was never known to fish. His house was ransacked, his LaSalle and other valuables taken. The car was spotted and chased almost to Canada. It spun out on a snowy curve where the suspected killer, Donald Dumont, a San Francisco private investigator, committed suicide. The Sheriff and his deputies are searching for Mrs. Engle. Dumont, Mr. And Mrs. Engle are believed to have been involved in embezzlement and had a falling-out."

#

The first Dr. Seuss book, published by Vanguard Press in 1937—"And to think I saw it on Mulberry Street," had been rejected by twenty-three other publishers.

#

# 7-FLIGHT OF FANTASY

Kurt had never considered himself a bore. He held that socks not lasting a lifetime were a great disappointment and caused one to lose faith in modern commerce. The shock when his wife wanted him to move his armchair from the middle of the room to the corner was overcome, but not during the first week.

"If I'd wanted it in the corner, I'd have moved it there twenty years ago," he'd told her. That seemed to satisfy her.    At least she shrugged her shoulders and walked away, never again to broach the subject.    Having seen this irrational side of her personality blossom so late in their twenty-five year marriage, he was less surprised when she packed her bags one bright summer day and left him with only a note,

"I've filed for divorce.    I'm going to find some excitement in my life while there's still time."

Well, she was at that age when women do such things.    It was part of life's cycle.    He didn't understand it, but he'd accepted it as one of the things that men weren't meant to understand.    Like why did some people phone, wait one ring, then hang up?    Since he never answered the phone the only thing more irritating was those who let the phone ring a thousand times before hanging up, finally deciding no one is going to answer. Well, the kids were gone; he was alone and facing one's birthday alone is one thing, spending it alone in an empty house is quite another.

That's why he decided to treat himself to a birthday present.    Two weeks in London.    Money was no real problem; he had the income from all those oil stocks he'd bought under the employer-matching fund.    Why not enjoy himself in the greatest city in the world?

*  *  *  *  *  *

The London bound Republic International Boeing 767 lazes over Nova Scotia when a terrorist group, using razor sharp laminated acrylic knives, forces access to the flight deck.    There isn't time to state their demands before an air marshal disarms one, shoots another.    The remaining two terrorists kill the entire flight deck crew before they too are overpowered.

The plane, caught in a hard banking turn to port is heading, via the polar route, toward Russia.    The chief steward asks frantically if anyone aboard can fly the plane. In business class, one grey haired man in conservative clothes, volunteers. Once he has a chance to view the massive array of controls and the attendant opportunity for error, he freezes, goes into shock and has to be sedated. Another man, an ex-USAF observation plane pilot thinks better of his raised hand. Kurt alone is willing to try. On the flight deck, he takes hands-on control and radios for assistance. A nearby Air National Guard F14 pilot overhears the mayday, notifies the nearest S.A.C. base, which relays it to civilian A.T.C.s. He swoops his Tomcat to a position where he can visually monitor the flight's progress.

A representative of Republic International comes on the radio, asks if Kurt is willing to try to bring the plane in. He says sure and he's given heading, time and speed, control settings, and they wish him luck.

Kurt disengages the autopilot, turns onto the new heading, drops to the proper altitude and makes his statement of condition to the passengers. He ends with,

"I'm authorizing the chief steward to serve free champagne to all passengers."

Back at F.A.A. headquarters, Kurt's qualifications are scrolled onto the computer screen. He holds a private pilot's license to fly twin-engine propeller-driven aircraft only. The A.T.C. and Republic executives panic.

On board, another call is put out for a more qualified pilot; the same two again show little promise. The first refuses to take the responsibility, the other, unsure of his ability claims failing eyesight, but will co-pilot if needed. Kurt, already in contact with the Omaha Naval Ordinance Disposal Depot, requests rerouting to Chicago. Chicago A.T.C., fearing a crash tries to divert them to a less crowded facility. Kurt responds with,

"My aircraft is in perfect flying condition with three hundred souls aboard. O'Hare has the best emergency provision in the event of an unfortunate occurrence and if not the plane should better be able to continue, with a fresh crew, to its original destination."

With the ATC's guidance, he lands the plane without incidence, but is held on the taxiway by an alarmed tower. One steward panics, opens an emergency door, lets down the slide and exits with three others. Two sustain injury in the dark. Kurt has the slide cut loose and he taxis to the nearest dock for the safe offloading of any passengers wishing to deplane.

He brings the plane to within inches of a perfect docking. The plane empties to the flash of TV cameras and a barrage of questions from newsmen.

The media people wait with anxious excitement, as Kurt, the last to emerge, seems surprised at his reception. TV monitors title him <u>Hero of the Year</u>. The president of Republic is on his way to present in person, a good citizenship plaque. Kurt is given a complimentary suite at the O'Hare Regency. The Mayor presents him a trophy for showing the indomitable American spirit and a key to the city for selecting Chicago, "the center of the free world." Kurt accepts shyly; showers and has dinner with Miss Illinois.

* * * * * *

The next morning TV cameras are transmitting, as personal interviews are set-up with Good Morning America. Kurt refuses, also cancels the Oprah, Regis & Kelly and Today shows. He goes instead to the public library. The president of Republic arrives at noon and arranges a banquet in Kurt's honor.

After dinner another award is given and Kurt makes his little speech on national TV.

"This, my fiftieth birthday, is a very special day for me.    I extend my thanks to Chicago for its friendly welcome, the Regency for its gracious hospitality, and the news media for making me out a role model when I deserve no such honor."

Seemingly unintimidated by the lights and cameras, he finishes with a special thanks to Republic for setting him upon a new career.    The president seems unsure of his meaning.    One of the reporters asks.

Kurt replies,    "According to labor contracts existing between all American International Air carriers, I expect to enjoy my new position as Flight Commander."    He explains in further detail.

"No federally chartered line may employ anyone to fly their aircraft who is not a full-time, regularly assigned pilot with said company.    Therefore, since I was asked to take over the controls by an officer of Republic, it was an implied offer of employment.    I accept, and while terms were not negotiated at the time, the union has strict guidelines.    Only aircraft commanders with proper credentials may become members, except for the grandfather clause which, at the time of employment recognizes a pilot as qualified."

"But, you're past the age of employment. Our upper limit is 49."

"My exact age when you hired me."

"Well, you have no experience in airliner command."

"I spent twenty-five years as an oil wildcatter.    I've flown into weather that would scare a polar bear, landed on ice floes that would have puckered Evel Knievel's every orifice; extracted drinking water from succulents on the Gobi dessert and brought a whole pumping crew through a middle-east shooting war without a scratch. I've negotiated with Central American leaders for the extraction of oil and safe conduct for Americans caught in an unfriendly country after our Embassy claimed impotence."

Republic goes into a flap. They try to weasel out by stating that Kurt had no right to endanger the craft and passengers by his lack of experience.

He retaliates with, "There were two other qualified individuals aboard, but they refused the responsibility. I landed the ship without sustaining damage to property or injuries to passengers or crew."

"Not true, there were two injuries during the landing."

"Because four of your trained stewards lost their cool and abandoned ship."

"Well, you had no right to cut the slide or bring the plane to the dock."

"It's an aircraft commanders' responsibility to issue orders to the crew and make such on-board decisions as will best provide safety and security for his passengers, ship and crew."

"You had no authorization to issue champagne at the airline's expense."

"O.K. I'll pay for that myself. Let's see, I ordered Totts. It's the best of the three champagnes you offer."

Totts calls, offers Kurt free champagne for the rest of his life, and pays for that served on board. The airline recants, offers him employment as ground personnel.

"Union rules state that a lesser position must be mutually agreeable to all parties and will still command the higher salary. I don't wish a ground job. I have great confidence in Boeing, the 767 and Republic."

"But you're not F.A.A. multi-engine certified."

"I've flown Ag-Cats, worn out C54's, F80's, Catalinas, Huey choppers and others too numerous to mention. You can put me through a crash course."

"We have no openings for Aircraft Commander right now."

"I know of at least two.   I saw to the removal of the bodies myself.   I can also help you with your security problems."

## EPILOG

Republic makes the best of a bad situation.   They not only hire Kurt as a full time Captain, give him upgrade training to multi-engine and pay him top wages (Union seniority rules state not only time- in-grade but age also dictates that increases be paid a man fulfilling a commensurate role and demand regular raises and company seniority).

He's put on the Paris to London route and becomes an instant international celebrity.   With a flat in Mayfair, an apartment in Paris and more money than he can spend; Kurt is an inspiration to other senior citizens who feel themselves powerless non-entities, a challenge to many single stewardesses.   His success is, however, a constant irritation to his ex-wife who finds life in a rented, singlewide mobile home in a run-down trailer park in Akron not exactly the excitement she'd had in mind.

#
Dr. Seuss' "Green eggs and Ham," has sold
over six million copies.
#

# 8-JUST LIKE ME

With chest-swelling pride, I receive the news that my first granddaughter will be named after me. The anticipation holds me in its grasp with arms of loving warmth.

Little Alice will grow up learning that the most important thing in life is to care for your children. Nothing must <u>ever</u> be allowed to come before them or interfere with building their character. I am serenely comforted to know that she will follow in my footsteps.

I'm truly sorry, however, that I'd never had time to develop a rapport with Margaret's husband.
Now that they are planning the future with the first little addition to their family, it won't be possible.

I so enjoyed the ride through such wild Idaho country, country I'd never expected to see. These beautiful virgin woods, so dense that the overhead canopy keeps sunlight from ever reaching the needle-covered ground and makes it hard to distinguish dawn from sundown. Though I do wish they had left me a blanket, even without snow or wind, the night is sure to be quite chilly. I did as much for my mother.

#
Over two hundred million Dr. Seuss books have
been sold.
#

# 9-THERE'S POWER IN CHICKEN BLOOD

*N.Y.P.D.-Central Manhattan-Homicide Squad*

"Have you got her?"

"She's a victim, Lieutenant. I've told you that from the beginning."

"Have you GOT her, Detective Woodruff?"

"Yes, but…"

"No buts, stay on top of her until you bring her to trial on Monday. If you lose her, you'll be in Jersey counting ducks for the Fish and Game with a clipboard instead of a side arm. Now get otta' my office."

"Does she suspect we're on her?"

Charlie, my partner and young mother drags me off before my retort gets me a reprimand or worse.

"No, it's better this way. Can you pull this one alone, partner? She asks. "My nine-month old is sick."

"Sure, go ahead, what's my time, my whole life worth anyway?"

"Oh, now don't sulk. I know how that "stay on top of her" must have had your shorts in a bunch. You can create your fantasies about her in private and not have to audibilize them to me. Until tomorrow, that is."

So alone, slumped in my car seat, drinking bitter, cold coffee from a tooth-marked Styrofoam cup, I watch Celeste Julliene enjoy La Boef's turtle soup, rack of lamb and cherries jubilee.

*Damn, she sure knows how to spend the D.A.'s budget. I wonder why no wine. Oh, Napoleon Brandy aperitif.*

I'm ready to move at the breath of danger, but so far it's only the four lotharios who try to insinuate themselves into the empty chair at her table. Not unexpected with such an exotic and beautiful brunette obviously dining alone.

Normally, a witness in danger behaves in a precise and proscribed manner.   Even with protecting agents watching for any alarm, they still never leave themselves open to attack, as does this woman.

*She's either failed to recognize the danger or she's the coolest character I've ever seen.   A very visible target, she shows no sign of stress.*

Hours later, I park across the street and with binoculars, I watch as she enters her apartment.   Journal at hand, I settle down for an all night vigil.

*Fri.  8-28  19:27* She arrived home, showered, brushed her hair and carried a book to bed.   All quiet on the western front.  J.A.W.

*Sat. 8-29 06:03* She's wearing a hot pink workout-suit that must have been pulled on only with liberal amounts of talcum and complete oxygen deprivation. J.A.W.

*Sat. 8-29 08:12* She took vitamins, drank scalding hot coffee, showered and dressed in some wraparound thing of dark blue velvet, the color of her eyes.

*It might have been demure, except for exposing legs that, start at the floor and rise to the clouds.*

She worked at her computer and listened to music.

*I wonder if her wardrobe contains anything not proper for a playboy centerfold. . J.A.W.*

*Sat.  8-29  19:09* She had shrimp scampi and vermicelli sent in from Antonio's on 14th, drank Pinot Noir (California label). J.A.W.

*Sat.  8-29  20:02* She watched PBS, Gershwin Revisited, narrated by Bernstein and ignored several phone calls. J.A.W.

*Sat. 8-29 21:03* She read, finished the Pinot Noir, exercised and went to bed.

*And I fight stress with weak, tasteless coffee, a cold, soggy hot dog, and a three-year-old Reader's Digest.* J.A.W.

Charlie relieved me at 22:00. J.A.W.

*Sun. 8-30 06:15* She repeated yesterday's boring routine (according to Jeff's report). C.I.L.

*I can imagine his frustration having to watch her exercise. Rough on the libido.*

*Sun. 8-30 17:09* This is total boredom.   She shows no inclination to leave the apartment.   Serious case of cabin fever for me though. C.I.L.

*Sun. 22:00* Jeff relieved me. C.I.L.

*Mon. 8-31 07:12* She's up, dressed and ready for court.

*I'm sure court is not ready for her.*   C.I.L./J.A.W.

*Mon. 8-31 07:19* She's wearing a white turtleneck under a cranberry suit of some kind of shiny material with matching shoes.   Her long, glossy black hair tucked under a white, Cossack–style, fur hat gives her height she doesn't need.   We'll pick her up on the street and escort her in.   She comes out into bright sunlight and pulls on goggle-style sunglasses that hide her azure-eye movement. J.A.W.

Charlie climbs out of the car and approaches, "Miss Julliene, I'm Charlene.   My partner, Jeff Woodruff, and I will see you safely to your testimony."

Celeste frowns as if Charlie had been told to polish the family silver, and forgetting her lowly station, has now spoken directly to her betters.   Without a word, she takes the front seat and I start from the curb, almost forgetting Charlie.  My mind is on something else.

*I'm taking this woman to a confrontation with the most dangerous man on the Eastern Seaboard.   I don't know enough about her to tell, but I'm guessing she's more nervous than she seems.*

61

With her eyes fixed on the horizon, we arrive on time, suffering only normal traffic glitches. Passing all the regular checks and rechecks, metal detectors, identity verifications, retinal scans and proffers of coffee, etc., we settle into a tiny, windowless and thankfully, intimate room. Up close, I spot the first sign of stress--a tiny twitch at the corners of her mouth and the constant twisting of a diamond ring on her right hand. The report says she's Puerto Rican, but she could pass for French, Portuguese, Creole or a few other ethnic origins.
She's lost any accent, probably due to her expensive Connecticut private school education.

*It won't help her blend into the affluent white community now. She's promised to testify against a gang lord. Will she ever be safe?*

My beeper vibrates. "Miss Julliene, the court is ready for you now, if you please."

She's led out with the demeanor and erect stature that Marie Antoinette must have carried as she casually strolled to the guillotine.

The judge instructs the jury that the testimony they are about to hear will be short and contain only questions agreed to by both defense and prosecution. The defendant Lex, snarling and in chains, is brought in. Celeste is sworn in and the first question is put to her by the District Attorney. "Do you recognize the defendant?"

She removes large-horn rimmed glasses from her purse. In place, they make her look like the comic book character, Henry Hawk.

*But a most beauteous hawk if ever there was one.*

She shoves her head forward and squints as if the end of her nose is out of focus. "May I approach the defendant a little closer, please?"

"If you must."

Carrying her purse as a security blanket, she approaches the accused. With intent, she takes a vial from her bag. In one motion, she uncorks and throws the entire contents, covering Lex's face and chest in chicken blood. She then spews her rebuke directly into his face.

"You vile creature, you murdered my brother because you thought he had overheard you speak of other killings. I can testify only to the murder you committed in my presence."

Casting aside the phony glasses and calmly, hips swaying, she returns to the witness box. Lex is led off, screaming and foaming at the mouth. Court is adjourned for the day. I escort Celeste home.

## Central Lock-up

Pacing his cell, an already nervous Lex finds a chicken feather tipped in blood. His sister, Gina arrives and while searching her purse for her visitor's pass she finds a bloody feather. She grows more furious by the minute, forced to wait two hours in a concrete cell that smells of sweat, stale cigarette smoke, urine and Lysol. They express their disgust at the lack of fairness accorded organized crime members. An unsympathetic sub-assistant D.A. finally hears their complaints.

"You want protection from what, a chicken missing a couple of feathers?"

## Celeste's Apartment

Alone but for Beethoven, Celeste orders from Orleans on the Wharf grilled salmon and wild rice. I drink weak, tepid coffee and watch from across the street. I find no comfortable position for my six-foot frame in the front seat of this Ford Taurus. Neither I, nor the uniform on stakeout at the rear alley, record any action throughout the night.

Lex, in a state of apoplexy shouts. "That witch has put a curse on me."

From his guard, "Don't be ridiculous: there are no witches."

Hyperventilating, Lex refuses to listen. "I'm Greek and we know of such things."

Lex is finally able to relax, "Better Living Through Chemistry" the prison doctor has given him a massive tranquilizer dose, but his olfactory senses unaffected by the drug, he notices a repulsive odor and finds a white gritty substance on the bars of his cell. A lab tech recovers samples of the chicken guano and several long grey hairs.

### *N.Y.P.D.-Central Manhattan-Homicide Squad*

With news of Lex's near total collapse, the question in the squad room is: where was Celeste? The Lieutenant swivels and points at me

"Get her apartment bugged. Fast! Let's see if she's really gone over to the dark side."

On stakeout, while attentively watching her apartment, I answer my cell phone.

"Yeah, she's in her recliner reading. Been there or working at her computer all the time."

Celeste, as if knowing that I'm on surveillance duty, and probably guessing her phone is tapped, makes no calls, takes none. Her movements in front of the uncurtained windows are witnessed, except when she takes items from a closet and puts on a C.D. playing typing sounds. Or when she pushes back her recliner and adjusts a long, dark-haired wig over the back of the chair to be viewed from the street.

Returning to her limousine after a lonely Saturday night dinner, Gina, is surrounded, verbally abused and tousled by a watching crowd of sign-carrying protesters. Holding the car door open, the chauffer sees blood staining the entire front of her thousand-dollar designer dress. She's casually pronounced dead by the bored E.M.T.'s. The investigation team calls, Lt. Wells. He gets me on my cell phone.

"Jeff, bring her in."

"Who?"

"You know who, the…witch."

"You don't mean that, Lieutenant."

"Serious as cancer. If you own a crucifix, wear it and stuff your pockets with garlic."

Celeste enters the interrogation room and the Lieutenant puts the question to her. "What's your connection to Gina's murder?"

"None. And I only know to whom you refer because I heard her name on the radio. Maybe she committed suicide."

"No, she was murdered."

"Well, she was probably as evil as her brother, so the world has suffered no great loss."

"Where were you at the time?"

"You'll have to tell me when it happened, before I can say."

"It was 9:30 tonight. Only a half dozen blocks from your place."

"Hum, it used to be a decent neighborhood. I suppose I will have to move."

"Your alibi, Miss Julliene?"

"Am I a suspect in this matter, Lieutenant?"

"Not yet."

"Well, let me see. I had dinner sent up about six, worked until after eleven and then went to bed. I was alone all that time, so I guess I have no alibi. It's a good thing I'm not a suspect."

A uniformed officer draws the Lieutenant into the hall. "The trial's suspended until further notice."

Charlie brings more bad news. "There are no good prints, but they're checking DNA of a grey hair they found caught in the wooden stake murder weapon."

The Lieutenant turns to me. "We need to compare it to hers."

I bristle. "We'll need a court order for that."

"Not if she gives a sample willingly."

"Why would she do that, unless she's innocent? And you know she is--I'm her alibi. She was in the apartment all night. Your bug will have her typing into her computer."

"Get me a hair sample, Jeff. Charm her if you have to."

Charlie tries to hide a grin with only limited success. Celeste unquestioningly offers a long, rich, vibrant dark hair sample.

### N.Y.P.D.-Central Manhattan-Homicide Squad

A white-smocked lab tech reads the results to Lt. Wells, "It's a close match, but the color is all wrong. Hers is jet black with traces of coconut shampoo. The crime scene hair and the hair from the cell are both grey, have dandruff and are identical. But they're all similar."

"What the hell does that mean?"

"It could be from her mother, but I'd say this is from a woman at least sixty years old, her grandmother, say. Only...her mother's been dead three years and her grandmother died when your suspect was ten. She has no other living relatives."

66

"Find out where the grandmother's buried."

The tech smiles. "Dead end (no pun intended). She was cremated and her ashes sent back to Porto Rico. Lex said she was a witch. Maybe the grandmother's spirit came back and….okay, just tryin' ta help."

"Yeah, I'm sure the D.A. will thank you personally. Maybe even let you repeat it to the jury yourself."

Charlie jumps up points to a glossy print. "Hey, these crime scene photos, I could swear…doesn't that look like our little miss Hokum in the background?"

They crowd around, nearly spilling their coffees on one another.

I shake my head in disbelief. "You're kidding. That woman's much shorter and has grey hair."

Charlie smiles. "She's not wearing five inch heels with her hair piled high atop her head. All that adds a foot to a person's perceived height. Besides, this woman is slouching, not sticking her boobs out, like you're used to seeing."

The Lieutenant sighs. "Okay, Charlie, get an enlargement made. Jeff, bring her back for more questions."

Celeste takes my arm as we enter the interrogation room. She smiles at the Lieutenant.

"What can you tell us about evidence implicating your grandmother in Lex's death?"

"I must finally tell the truth. You'd better write it down. I don't want to err in the details. I had suspicions that it was my grandmother, Emily. Now I'm afraid it must be true."

"Your grandmother's been dead for twenty years. Are you saying she's a zombie?"

"I'm Puerto Rican, not Haitian. We don't believe in voodoo."

"Lex accused you of being a witch, are you?"

"Do you believe in Santa Claus and the Easter Bunny as well?"

"I didn't <u>say</u> I believed it."

"If I said I was a witch, you'd rightfully put me in a rubber room."

"Then how do you explain it?"

"I don't.   But if you believe in reincarnation, there is an island theory that when a sin is too egregious to be tolerated, a past loved one may invest their soul in the body of a living being in order to bring about justice."

"And you expect us to accept that?"

"No, of course not.   I merely offer a possible extension of your paranormal scenario."

"Boss, the sheriff just called.   Lex was just found dead in his cell.   Signs indicate asphyxiation.   Suicide is extremely likely."

The Lieutenant paces as I read the M.E.'s report.

"He suffocated, and no marks were found on the body.   They think he held his pillow to his face until he died.   With his ranting about the witch thing they'd transferred him to a windowless isolation cell.   With the door tightly sealed, it might have been an accident, except the fresh air system never quit.   And with the cell always individually guarded, we'd never prove murder."

"She could have used the roof access and crossed to the adjacent building."

"The manager has the only key to the roof's padlock."

"And she killed him how?"

"Maybe she goes invisible and snuck right past you."

"Even if she did get out, you're saying she has unlimited access to our jail system?"

"I never said it was a perfect theory."

## Celeste's Apartment

Celeste flushes a padlock key down the toilet and with both the black wig that created her recliner alter ego and the grey wig she wore while killing Gina in the sink, she uses a match to turn them into a pile of grey ashes. The CD of typing sounds, she breaks into tiny pieces which she distributes to the wind gusting past her bathroom window. Lastly, she removes and burns the last of her grandmother's hair from the Cameo locket at her neck. Her computer dings and she reads the incoming Email before erasing it.

"That substance you told me of left no trace."

As she's returning a Cryogenics book to a packed top shelf, she removes the bookmark indicating the paragraph that warns about the dangerous misuse of carbon dioxide (dry ice).

> "Even short time exposure is extremely dangerous in a confined space as it consumes oxygen. A person can lose consciousness and die in minutes if adequate ventilation is not provided. The result would bear all the signs of a simple suffocation."

I knock and she invites me in. Accepting my presence in due course, she retires to her bedroom to change.

I make myself comfortable and from the sofa ask, "So how'd you do it?"

"Do what?"

"I know <u>why</u>, I just don't know <u>how</u>."

With her long hair tied back with a simple ribbon, her body fighting containment by a purple velvet lounging robe, its movement restricted only by a thick satin sash, the knot of which looks extremely insecure, she sashays her way to a hidden bar.

Retrieving ice and soda from the cooler, she adds Cutty Sark to two glasses, undulates her way to the couch and with a hungry python movement slithers down beside me.

I sip my drink as she explains. "With me as the only eye witness, the judge would surely have granted him bail. Why wouldn't I just wait to ambush him on the street? I mean if I was going to kill him, why do it where I would surely be caught?"

"You probably had a conspirator's help."

"I'm just a humble girl from a poor fishing village. What do I know of these things? Although, island people, all being related in some fashion, I suppose a distant possibility might exist that someone, unknown to me, saw the injustice and decided, on their own, to seek closure."

"The same guard on duty both when the feather was found and during Lex's death is of Puerto Rican ancestry."

"And have you found any connection between this person and myself?"

"No. But you were behind both deaths. Gina, I understand. It's retribution. He killed your brother so you put his sister in the ground, and Lex, well, this witch story filling the front pages should keep his superstitious gang from retaliating. Besides, they're as happy to be as rid of him as are we." I down my drink. "We'll never prove it and even if the case made it to court, you'd skate. Probably take the city for millions. I'm your alibi. You knew all along I'd been watching you from the car."

We both stand. She smiles, but remains silent.

"If you say anything incriminating, I'll be obliged to reveal it to my boss."

Placing her body in intimate contact with me at all the strategic places, her soulful kiss offers me her gratitude.

Back in the car, Charlie gives me a searching look.

"You can't really believe she's innocent?"

"Without proof to the contrary, the presumption of innocence prevails."

"So, you gonna hook up with her or what?"

"Are you kidding? She'd eat me alive."

"I thought that's what all you guys want."

"Not this time."

#

Remember, when enjoying the Florida or
Mexican beaches during spring break that
even though they may smell alike the coconut
oil suntan lotion goes ON the body and the
Pina-Colada goes IN the body. After a couple
of glasses one tends to confuse the two.

#

# 10-A STIRRING IN THE BRUSH

*Twilight is gone; in another half hour it'll be pitch black, another moonless night. Late fall is like that on Battle Mountain, Nevada. The grouse are scratching for seeds in the sand and the smell of wildflowers, still wet from the afternoon shower, is heavy on the air. Crickets, starting their evening serenade, almost make this wonderland come alive. It'll be hard to find me in the dark*

*Coyotes need very little light, and I hear them howling. They move almost silently, when scavenging. But I've hunted the high desert sagebrush country long enough to detect even their soft footpads in the dust. I hear them now, stirring in the brush. Will my brother Charlie get back in time to save my leg?*

No. That was 1937 and I was fourteen. I'd slid on the shale and broken my femur on a boulder.

Now, my jeep has hit a land mine, rolled over and trapped my leg--the same leg--under the weight of the engine. I've heard coyotes will chew off their own leg to escape a trap. I'd do the same, if I had anything sharp, I have my bayonet and it's fixed to my Garrand. Problem is, it's forty inches away and my reach is only thirty-seven inches. This is not Battle Mountain, nineteen-thirty seven; this is Tarawa and it's November twenty-third, nineteen forty-three. The stirring in the brush is not coyotes that kill quickly by slashing your throat; it's what's left of the Jap infantry. They take no prisoners, and they're masters of many slow death methods.

#

What's worse than learning that your wife is
having an affair with the pool boy?   Knowing
that you don't have a pool?
No, finding out that she's put you in hock for
eighty thousand for a pool so she can be up
front about her affair with the pool boy.

#

# 11-A TIME PAST

"Uncle Mark, how come your barn has such a small door?"

"Well, when my father bought this abandoned building it wasn't a barn.   It was part of a large community.   He got it cheap, 'cause there wasn't no use for it no more.   The town wasn't no more.   Mostly the people wasn't no more."

"What's a town, uncle?"

"That's where people used ta live, back when they had jobs and owned property.   Those days they had houses and cars and animals.   They din't live in the woods like now.   'Course they was lots more of 'em then. That was 'fore folks even had registration numbers, let alone wearing 'em tattooed on their foreheads.   In those old times, there were separate countries and individual governments.   I don't 'member it, but my dad used ta tell me about how things were, twenty year ago."

"But, then why…"

"Now that's enough ancient history.   We're almost out of gruel; I need ta get down to the Consolidation for our weekly allotment.   And you'll have to go to the creek for water before curfew."

"Okay."

"Help me carry this wooden beam outside. We'll cut it up for firewood. Careful now, that cross piece makes it hard to maneuver. Like you said, this door is small."

"What kind of a building is this, Uncle and what's this thing we're moving?"

"It's just the shell of a building now, used to be something called a church. We already burned up all the seats. Those days people believed in God. And this thing with a cross beam has something to do with a guy they called Jesus."

"Oh, I remember some old folks talking about him."

Outside, on the cracked stucco wall, a carved sign, swinging from the only remaining nail, hangs the church dedication date of 2010.

#
I can't understand why my 80-year college
reunion was so poorly attended.
#

# 12-BERLIN 1938

On the outskirts, in a small protestant church the opening prayer is finished, a beloved hymn has been sung and the ceremony of Communion is about to begin. The congregation as one squirms as nervously as prey knowing that a predator lies in wait and there is no place safe to hide. With a shaking hand atop his Bible, the minister tries to ignore the young steel, blue-eyed blond man in form fitting tailored black uniform standing ramrod straight against the back wall. He's not a member of the congregation. Everyone knows him and why he's there, but none dare acknowledge his presence. The ushers pass the bread from one row to the next. At

74

each successive aisle the silver trays are as full as when started, the same with the wine.   Then they come to a middle-aged man in shiny, worn, blue serge suit long out of fashion.   He quietly takes bread and when the wine comes he drinks.   No one turns; looks or whispers to a neighbor, but all know what has happened, even those in the pews ahead.

Only the blond man in back moves.   He makes notes in a small leather notebook, returns it to the pocket of his silver-trimmed shirt and leaves.

The next Sunday, the spot occupied for thirty years by the middle-aged man and before him, his fore fathers is empty.   No one has seen him, no one has asked or mentioned about his empty spot or seems to miss his close-cropped gray head or the clink of his few pfennigs in the collection plate.

The following week, with no communication among themselves, the congregation is in place.   The blond man, again at his spot, pencil and notebook ready.   This time as Communion is served, the full trays lessen as they make their way toward the back.   The man, confused, sees the trays.  All are empty.

The word spread, first among the small churches, gradually worked its way to the larger, more traditional congregations.

Did it change the outcome of the next few years? No, but I think it effected the lives of those committed individuals.

#

When decanting that seven thousand dollar
bottle of 1927 Chateau Montrachet as the local
TV station films the event, remember it's not
classy to chug-a-lug from the bottle.

#

75

# 13-COMMUTE

"You know it takes time, John."

"But, Warden, the Governor <u>must</u> commute my sentence. The penalty's not right, it's not just."

"Your lawyer is checking with Constitutional experts to find a loophole, but…"

"He's been trying since before the trial. Nobody wants to get involved, but the whole world knows the bizarre nature of the charge."

"Well, John, when you planned this you knew there might be repercussions."

"That's no excuse for making me a scapegoat just because I'm a Republican and he's a Democrat. What I did can't demand such a penalty."

"Well, it's an election year and the public mandate was clear."

"But without that organ, I'd be dead in another year. As it is, I should live out a full and healthy life, collect my Social Security and pension."

"When you were diagnosed with a failing kidney five years ago, you were put on the waiting list for a donor kidney."

"Yeah, number 1004, now I'm down to 675. With luck, in four or five years I might get one. It might even be a perfect match. Of course it won't matter because I'll already be dead."

"But, John, what you did, it's…it's unnatural, it's immoral."

"Sure, you can say that, it's not <u>your</u> life at stake. Everything would have been fine if the D. A. had just followed precedent. No one's ever been imprisoned for this before."

"You know, because of the statute you were convicted under, you're famous. You'll go down in history as setting new legal precedent."

"Thanks, that warms the cockles of my heart"

"I'm just trying to be empathetic."

"More like pathetic, I say."

"There's still a chance. We might hear at the last minute."

"Sure, I could win the lottery too. It's not right to jump from a misdemeanor to a felony just for mutilating a corpse. It isn't fair."

"That's an oversimplification, John."

"The scientists developed the technique, I simply put it to practical use."

"You killed and took all the usable parts."

"They were legally mine, clones were declared non-persons by Obama back in 2011."

"Here they come now. Talk to the Padre, he'll help with your torment, maybe give you absolution."

"We're both Catholic, Warden. You know there's no hope for me. If they'd convicted me of murder there might have been a chance. But since I was found guilty of suicide, I'll go straight to hell."

The iron gate squeaks open and as the entourage enters, a guard hands the warden a note. He reads it and smiles.

"Good news, John. You've been moved up, you're now number 666 on the waiting list."

The priest makes the sign of the cross as John, his head shaved and pants leg slit is led crying and screaming from the cell.

Unless you're Superman, it's best to wear your
underwear beneath your clothes.

## 14-DON'T NEVER MESS WITH A SOBER IRISHMAN

Paddy walked confidently into the Third Precinct Police Station, asked the procedure for witnessing a possible illegal event. Taking the forms to the long grey-metal table and using the chained pen he filled out the form as completely as possible and returned it to the desk. As the Sergeant casually read the report his eyes widened. He pushed an under-counter switch with his knee and inhaled deeply. He looked down at the short stocky, redheaded, well dressed, but trend-confused man standing with 27-inch biceps crossed over a size 46-chest.

"You say you witnessed these people putting some twenty-odd large white powder filled plastic bags into their new Mercedes Benz, and you got the license number? Are you claiming a reward?"

"No, sir, just doing what any socially conscious citizen should do. The car's still parked in front of 415 Park Avenue. They spilled some of the powder. If you hurry, you might get a sample before the wind scatters it."

He smiled and walked out without a backward look. At the corner, he dropped coins into the slot and made phone calls to the local TV stations and newspapers.
He'd been especially careful not to be seen loading the bags of powdered sugar into the car trunk and then sprinkling a different powder behind the car.

From the dark back seat of his Toyota RAV4 he watched as three patrol cars double-parked and uniformed precinct members tested as positive the powder from the street. The hand waving and radio conversation was followed shortly by an unmarked car with two plain-clothes detectives carrying subpoenas. They flashed gold badges at the doorman, and entered the high-rise. When they returned, leading the handcuffed, distinguished couple, newspaper reporters and TV cameramen were filling the sidewalk and recording the event.

When the open trunk disclosed the plastic bags, the pair were helped into the back of a cruiser and driven off. Paddy waited until an NYPD tow truck arrived to drag off the seventy thousand dollar sedan.

* * * * * *

The news of the arrest of Mr. and Mrs. Goodwin, owners and operators of multiple up-scale co-op apartment buildings in New York's fashionable east side was given top priority by all media.

* * * * * *

When the suspected cocaine was found to be sugar, the impound auto mechanics were told to tear the car apart. The only logical reason for that much sugar, the detectives deduced, was to cut dope. No other drugs were found in the vehicle and the Goodwins, after producing a one million dollar bond, were released from custody. When the only drugs found in their twelve-room penthouse were four ounces of marijuana, the Goodwins pled guilty of the misdemeanor and were given a ticket to appear for community service. They were allowed to recover their car, now in over six hundred disparate pieces.

* * * * * *

79

Paddy typed a second letter to the Goodwins, again requesting the return of his five thousand dollar deposit for the co-op apartment he'd chosen not to buy.

* * * * * *

Sorting their pile of mail on the forty thousand dollar, Duncan Fife desk took the Goodwins almost two hours. Paddy's letter, when read, was delegated to the circular file without a second thought.

* * * * * **

Paddy paid cash for the kiddy-porn dvd's and had the itemized receipt made out to Win Good. Wearing gloves, he dropped the manila envelope holding the dvd's into the "local" slot at the main Post Office. The widespread brass fasteners and the torn corner left agape, the overflowing package was sure to be damaged by the sorting equipment of the moving belt.

* * * * * *

As the ten-foot, hand carved solid teak doors were opened to them, Post Office Inspectors and vice cops entered the Goodwin's suite. The Goodwins were taken into custody for sex crimes.

* * * * * *

Questioning the arrest team, the captain got less than satisfactory answers. "You had no probable cause other than the torn envelope?"

"Cap, you know these perverts seldom confess, even when caught with the goods."

"They never acknowledged ownership of the tapes?"

"Naw, but who else'd pay for 'em, then have them mailed?"

80

"I don't know, but you'll have to release them."

The newspaper account of the sexual deviate arrest of the Goodwins commanded page one.   Page-seventeen carried the retraction of their drug arrest story.   Former friends now ignored them and they were treated to angry looks from neighbors.   The mail stack this time was substantially smaller than before, but the third letter down was from Paddy,

"May I express my personal sorrow over the troubles you continue to experience, but things like this often happen to those who ignore moral business protocol. Possibly even more travail will come.

Kind of like the plagues the Pharaoh suffered by acting improperly.  He should have let the Israelites go, or returned their good faith co-op deposits."

The Goodwins, after re-reading the note several times finally gained the insight to decipher the implied meaning.   They rebated Paddy's deposit with interest. Miraculously, from the exact date their check cleared, the Goodwins experienced no new legal problems. However, their property management empire had suffered a sixty percent drop, their legal defense cost them a million and a half dollars and the I.R.S., reviewing their last seven returns, disavowed six million in past tax write-offs.

#

If the lobster you ordered comes with a
disposable toilet seat cover in place of a bib it's
probably not a five star restaurant.

#

# 15-DANCING IN THE DARK

It's serendipity.    I knew <u>about</u> her, never expected to meet her.    Well, I haven't, yet.    The Atlantic City Hyatt Regency convention hall normally, on a Friday evening, is chaos, with stallholders unpacking their wares. Many vendors use balloons, flashing lights, hokie carnival hype to attract crowds (skimpily-clad young, attractive models, handing out free coupons).    When I first notice her she's in a tailored black suit that might be conservative, but her lush curves leave little to the imagination.    It isn't her pulchritude that first catches my eye; oh hell, sure it is.    But the author whose book and conference schedule she's hawking really draws my continued attention.    Finishing our displays at the same time, she saunters toward the Buffet and I head to my room.    While awaiting room service to bring my dinner, I Google her and get the information I'm seeking, maybe hoping not to find.

Saturday at the continental breakfast, my attempt at contact blocked, I take yogurt, coffee and a banana into the conference room and settle behind my booth.

My "Brad Talbott--Security to the Stars," display immediately attracts people obviously unable to afford my services.    Each time I'm free, she's occupied.

*The entire morning gone and I've not even made eye contact.  Lunch break, when they close the arcade floor to allow booth holders a short respite.  Surely I'll manage contact by then.*

Checking for messages at the front desk, I spot the phalanx of badge toters.

*FBI or similar ilk, not locals.*

They question the manager in subdued tones, but I hear enough.    They're asking about Dana Albright--her room number, booth location, if she is on the premise and no they don't want her paged.

"She can be found, most likely, at her booth during the afternoon session."

I take a short cut through service corridors and catch her alone, waiting for the side doors to open. I don't hesitate; grasping her elbow I pull her unceremoniously into an alcove among dirty dish-filled carts. Her mouth opens in what is intended as a scream. My words stop that in mid-inhale.

"They're at the front desk. They're holding local, federal and international warrants. They'll be watching your room and your booth. Once you show your face you'll be cuffed and in the back seat of a black sedan before you ever see a badge. You won't get a phone call and you can forget bail."

"Who are you and what the hell are you talking about?"

"I have the security services booth across from you. But the important question is, do you want to get clear of this now, or will you march into a cell with your head held high, proclaiming your innocence?"

"I don't know what you're…"

"Save it, Dana. I know your scam almost as well as you. Your books are counterfeit and the seminar tickets are fake. You're grossing forty G's on these weekend affairs, so it's profitable enough that you're convinced you can go on forever. Today you've hit the end of your string. Without my help you're trapped."

Her green eyes showing her involuntary acceptance of an unwanted truth, she makes a lightning decision.

"And how precisely can you help me?"

"First, I'll have your room cleaned out. When you don't return to your booth, they'll check your room. While they're there I'll have your booth cleared."

"And where will I be all this time, hiding in a laundry sack?"

"Not unless you've a taste for such things. You'll be in my room, out of sight. I'll be at my booth watching things unravel."

"How will you...?"

I guide her into an empty service elevator and take it up to nine.

"What's your room number?"

"Seven-0-nine."

At the maid's station, I phone the Bell Captain's desk.

"Miss Albright has received bad news. She's taken an emergency flight home. Please have her personal belongings packed and put into hotel storage. She'll pick them up in a week or so. Just total her credit card and send a copy to her office, thank you."

Guiding her into my room, 902, I take the receiver off the hook and show her how to place wedges around the door to prevent unwanted entry. I also give her a pager.

"This automatically scrambles voice transmission, so just speak normally. Don't use text and keep the ringer on silent mode. I'll do the same. Stay here and you'll be safe."

I get my first unhurried look at what I'd missed while she was behind her booth. From the neck up she was phenomenal, but from the shoulders down she's clearly more than a sub-compact or mini, but a full-sized luxury model with all the extra features you expect in a top of the line selection. Atop stiletto heels she's almost a match to my six feet, and every inch is packed with woman. More is not needed, but less would be criminal.

"They'll be watching all exits if they think I'm still here. How will I get out?"

"I've got that covered, but there's no time now to explain. I want to watch the booth as they make their next move. You can have my tuna sandwich. I didn't have time to eat."

"Thanks, but I had lobster and champagne for lunch."

I smile and slip out the door, changing the maid's sign to "Do Not Disturb." Back at my booth I watch the watchers trying unsuccessfully to seem unobtrusive, but clearly realizing their quarry may have slipped the trap. As they grow more restive, one or another responds to a shirt cuff or tie clip with the same results: a furrowed brow and darting eyes. When they depart enmass I call the Convention Chairman and reprise my "Miss Albright has been called away" story. I watch as her booth is stripped and her material placed in carts.

When the afternoon rush dwindles, I close my own booth and make my way to the hotel storage vault. From overhead I find the key that I know is there. Once inside, I locate her personal and seminar items and exchange the owner I.D. tags with ones giving my own room number. As the dinner crowd fills the lobby, I find a bored, slender chauffeur.

With a hundred dollar bill and whispered instructions I get the young man to follow me to my room. The clothes switch takes only a few minutes and from a bed sheet torn into a narrow strip, I stuff Dana's cascade of auburn hair into the homemade turban. Even sans makeup and wearing the chauffeur's uniform over her own clothes she wouldn't fool anybody up close, but with her cinnamon complexion and the pants covering her heels, she might pass casual inspection. The chauffeur, wearing my pastel vacation shorts and hibiscus sport shirt follows her out the side entrance. She holds the limo's back door for him, then takes the wheel; I follow in my own car.  The caravan travels three hundred yards to the Atlantis Casino parking lot where costumes are again exchanged.  When the chauffeur drives off with another hundred dollars, she climbs in beside me and we join the freeway traffic.

* * * * * *

Once we've bypassed New York City traffic I phone the hotel.

"This is Mr. Talbott, room 902.  I've been called away unexpectedly.  Please have my personal and booth items put into storage.  I'll later confirm the address for some and have the rest shipped to my home."

* * * * * *

Winding up the curved driveway, I stop beside a high brick wall.  I speak into a metal box and the iron gate slides open.  Inside the mini-mansion, while she looks around like a child on a first trip to Disneyland, I fax to the hotel, addressed labels for trans-shipment of her boxed material to a London address.  As she ends her tour at my side, I tell her the latest.

"I've sent your counterfeit merchandise to the author you've been pirating and had your personal belongings sent here."  As she screams her outrage, I calmly print copies of something from the Internet. "Well, you can probably stop them from shipping."

I hand her the printouts (want ads for entry-level stock-persons at a dozen companies).  "These companies all have an acceptance policy of hiring ex-cons.  When you get out of prison, you might check them first."

"What do you mean when I get out of prison?"

"They'll be tracking the books and nab you as soon as you try to claim your illicit merchandise.  All my efforts to save you will have been in vain."

The thoughts racing through her brain are clearly mirrored in her eyes.

"How do you know all this? About Ben Yamin's book? How did you figure I wasn't part of his entourage?"

"Several past clients had referred him to me. He knew that an employee had copied his new book and speaking engagement calendar and realized he needed security. You knew he'd be out of the country for three months and thought you were safe for that long. It's just lucky, my having the booth across from you."

"Yeah, lucky. Okay so how did you know about those service corridors at the hotel? I think you were stalking me."

"I worked there while a Princeton undergraduate."

Leaving her alone in my office, I see to dinner. Trying to access my computer, she gets only screen savers. In anger and frustration, finding valuable netsuke, she hides several in her purse. In the garage, she tries to start the car, but there's no ignition lock and the garage door won't open. She jumps when I lean over her skulking body. I smile.

"We're almost out of gas, you'll have to fill it up."

I start the car for her, adjust her seat, fasten her seat belt and harness, and open the garage door. She zooms down the driveway. I saunter after her. When she can't open the iron gate, the car quits. A robotic voice informs her that the police are on their way and that any damage she causes will be added to the grand theft auto charge. She can't get the doors or windows open. When I voice the command, the car door opens, but the seatbelt won't release and she's still trapped.

"I figured you were smarter than this. Why don't we return to the house and have a leisurely dinner while I notify the police of a false alarm?"

I hoped the dinner would be is as upscale as everything else her accusing eye has scanned.

* * * * * *

An ear-piercing sound reverberates in her head and rattles her teeth.

"What the hell is that?"

I answer over her bedside intercom.

"It's the computer alarm clock."

"Why is it going off in the middle of the night?"

"It's seven A.M."

"That's what I mean, make it stop."

"It stops when your feet hit the floor."

"Well, just unplug the damn thing."

"I can't. You're in the panic room; remember? No one can get in unless you release the internal security locks."

She slides one bare leg over the edge of the bed and the noise stops. It starts again as soon as she slips back under the covers.

"What the hell?"

"You can't trick it. It will stop while you shower, but if you get back in bed it'll start again."

"Damn."

* * * * * *

After a long, luxurious shower she dresses and goes through the litany of returning the computer-generated security room to stand-down mode and the one-ton door slides open. I'm standing there with two glasses of orange juice.

"Why on earth must you get up before civilization, you have to borrow fat back and chittlins from your nearest neighbor in the next county? Where are we anyway, Utah or the edge of the world?   Oh, wait, that's redundant."

"We're in New Hampshire and forty acres seem like more because of the heavy foliage."

She seems depressed, as if she wants to hit something, but can't find anything that might not hit back.

"What's wrong, bad hair day?"

"What's wrong with my hair?"

"Not a thing."

She smiles as if she's won the exchange, but unsure how.

\* \* \* \* \* \*

She doesn't ask directly about the almost inexhaustible and diverse security devices, but her memory banks record all that she sees.

*The main gate responds to his classic command of open sesame.   Retinal scanners operate the house entrances and a handprint sensor activates his command computer.   In the panic room--actually complete living quarters--at least the computer recognizes my voice, necessary to open the anti-tank and rocket-proof door. He has overrides on everything, but he didn't share them with me, I don't think he completely trusts me.   He told me about the tear gas dispenser to give me confidence. NOT! Surely any device he's made foolproof to <u>others</u>, <u>he</u> can defeat.*

I indicate no uneasiness at her taking every advantage to learn my operation, and that puts her into a state of disbelief.

*He must know I've been picking his brains to increase my obsessive compulsion for riches.   I've been here almost a month and he hasn't made a single pass at me.   He's not gay or the décor wouldn't be the bachelor pad it is.   So what gives?*

89

"Why are you doing this? What do you want from me?" You made me give back all my hard earned money. What did you get out of it?"

"We are all a work in progress. None of us is the person we were yesterday, nor the person we will be tomorrow. You've made some bad life-choices but I think you can correct them and finish the race with style."

"I haven't done so badly."

"That's what Dillinger thought as the lady in red led him from the Biograph Theater. There's no glory in running the first mile of a marathon. You have to finish the race to receive acclaim."

She retires to her own suite to consider her options.

* * * * * *

She brings two glasses of champagne into my bedroom, and with only the moonlight streaming through the wall of windows she curls onto the side of my bed. Even in the dim light that silhouettes her figure, it's clear that she's wearing only the skimpiest of black lace. In a soft, melodious, hopefully hypnotic voice she makes her sales pitch.

"O.K., here's the deal, you'll have to sign my pre-nup before I'll marry you."

"Who said I wanted to marry you?"

"Oh, your eyes gave you away that first time you dragged me into the corridor and since you kidnapped me, it's obvious even to your semi-sentient computer.

"What's that about a pre-nup?"

"There are a lot of minor details, but the important clause says if you are unable or unwilling to perform sex at least three times a day you must supply a doctor's written excuse."

I swallow both glasses of champagne and pull her atop my welcoming form.   Hopefully, these actions make my acceptance of her terms clear.

#

I can stand mid span on the Perrine bridge and
have no urge to jump with parachute, bungee
cord or just the desire to fly.   I love that about
myself.

#

# 16-HOLIDAY GREETINGS

The Twin Falls District Attorney, Chief of Police, County Sheriff and Homeland Security Representative all cluster around the railing of the County Courthouse rotunda and stare in amazement at the scene below.   In order, they voice their concern, advise, and fear.

"I hope he's been read his rights."

"If he makes any aggressive move taze him again. We don't want innocent civilian workers endangered, in the event he gets loose."

"He looks dangerous."

"Did you find any weapons of mass destruction on him?   Is he working alone or does it appear to be a foreign conspiracy?

Below, seventeen assorted officers of the law stretch their prisoner like an old-fashioned torture rack.   At their first frightening sight of this monstrous being, all witnesses shrink in revulsion.

"Lieutenant, I understand you caught him skulking around the Bickle Elementary School and he was wearing this elaborate disguise, clutching a bag of candy and carrying presents with which to entice the poor wretched little souls to join in his dastardly deeds?"

91

"Let me turn him loose mongst my jail population. He won't look so good, come morning."

"My men know how to treat a pedophile like this. They'll take him into the desert and…"

"If he had any chemicals or unidentified powders on him, around him, or anywhere he might have access, put him in a holding cell until the bomb squad gets here."

The white haired and bearded, rotund old man finally stops fighting his restraints, his red suit and black shiny boots have been torn off in the ensuing struggle and he finally has an opportunity to give his story. "It's December 21$^{st}$, I make my rounds to all the schools this time of the year, spreading joy and good cheer. It's a custom enacted all over the world."

"Lieutenant?"

"Must be some sort of evil sect, probably from southern California. In the parking lot he's got a sled with some kindda mules with horns. I figure he uses 'em to bait the poor innocent tykes. Had this notebook, too, classifin'em by who's been naughty an' who's been nice. Like he was planning to stalk some of the kids later."

"The evil creature must think we'd buy that kind of cult stuff. Here in Idaho, we respect religious and patriotic occasions, not that phony Scientology kinda stuff."

"If he ever serves his term in prison, take him to the border and turn him loose, let him try that nonsense someplace else. Like Utah, maybe."

#

It's mandatory on all Idaho freeways that any
skateboarder over the age of eighty must wear
a helmet.

#

# 17-I'D REALLY HAVE PREFERRED FISH

The service is impeccable, the hor-doevers are four star, the cocktails superb and the setting (an excellent wedding reception choice) is to die for. The endive and truffle salad the envy of any Gordon Ramsay restaurant, the turtle soup matchless and the tuber-rose table center pieces fill the air with a heady romantic fragrance and the sterling silver place settings sparkle from the candle lights. I am perhaps being unduly critical with the selection of Angus ball-tip roast as the selected entrée. I know it's not fitting to have chosen pork, turkey or even the plebian favorite, catfish, but there it is; I'd rather have had any of those. Unfortunately I wasn't on the menu selection committee.

Sure, I'm sleeping with the chapter president, so I might have exerted some influence, but I guess I just wanted my feelings to be considered without it becoming an issue. Oh, yes, he buys me a new expensive gown for all these occasions and always sends flowers and a limousine whenever he's unable to pick me up in person.

It's…just, well, with the fish I could have requested white wine. But I mustn't complain too strenuously, I chose to be here as an honored member, sitting at the head table. It matters not that I detest the pomp and circumstance that accompanies the introduction of a new convert to our flock. There they are now, center stage. She in black faille and he, the one I'd sworn to spend eternity with, as handsome as ever, in black cut-away.

With the smiles and in-drawn breath of the entire audience he bends over her neck and drinks--she swoons and he hurries back to the head table, bringing to me the silver chalice. I share the warm, fresh blood.

# 18-AUTOBIOGRAPHY

I was born at a difficult time in the history of the world.   Things would only get worse in the following years.  Depression lay heavy upon the land.   Winters were the hardest, with only enough income for a few scraps of stale bread and a bit of milk to sop it up and make an edible consistency.   There was no money left with which to buy coal.   In minus zero-degree weather, I could find an occasional lump alongside the tracks, though with fingers numb, they were hard to pick up. Evenings we would wear every bit of clothing we could find (threadbare and non-sex discriminating) and huddle together throughout the night.   Daytime we would stuff every loose scrap of paper we could find into our meager clothes and go out looking for any kind of work.

Soon I was old enough for school, and although smaller and less socially adept as the others, it opened, for me, a window onto the greater expanse of God's goodness.   There I learned to appreciate the song of birds and the gurgling of a brook, the smell of wildflowers or fresh pine pitch, the feeling of the spring breezes on my face.

My home life wasn't unusual, in that my relationship with my father was strained, although I adored and worshiped my mother.

Outside social pressures were creating a strong familial and patriotic pride, only to strengthen during my teen years.   I joined the army.   It enabled me to step from boyhood into adulthood. Here I learned to laugh, to develop a stronger resolution to my fellow man, to commit myself toward helping my country. Combat challenged my moral base. How could anyone see man's inhumanity to man and not question God's compassion for his greatest creation?

Later, while in a secure environment, I had the ability and inspiration to exercise an introspection that drove me to write my book. The book that would explain how man could end wars and live in peace with each other as individuals or as nations.

Now, after putting my thoughts and ideas to the test, I have proven the efficacy of my thesis. As I took the podium, I vowed to lead my country, my people, (this strong, united people) to the world eminence it deserves. Already, even though I hear only a small minority chant, in my heart, I knew that the cry would swell.

"Sig Heil, Sig Heil, Sig Heil, Sig Heil, Sig Heil, Sig Heil, Sig Heil."

#
My proctologist was the inspiration for Ian
Fleming's book, "Cold Finger."
#

# 19-ENJOYING AUTUMN IN THE MOUNTAINS

Almost dawn and the cans seem heaver than usual, even padded, the bar digs into my shoulders. If water is heavier then alcohol, why doesn't this feel lighter? Ten gallons seems like a hundred and eighty pounds, and commin' down this steep mountain grade isn't easy any time. Watching for loose shale, jinking around bushes, Southern white pine and their carpets of slippery needles makes it a whole 'nother game.    Partta the biggest distilled spirit business in the Smokey Mountains, I also watch for strangers roamin' the country.    I'm concentrating on balance and footwork, when I feel the sting of a Scottish Thistle on my leg.

Then I hear the rattle as he hits me again.    Damn, I jerk my leg and the heavy cans tumble down the hill and burst open on the rocks.    My ever-at-hand bowie knife is ready, but too slow.    Rattler safety is: Step 1-Kill the snake: 2-look for it's mate.    I can't, but I can attend the wounds, four punctures I could cover with a poker chip. With one hand I open my water bottle and squeeze it dry; with the other, I make the needed X cuts over each strike. As the blood oozes, I draw the poison into the bottle and use my belt as a tourniquet.    When my count gets to sixty, I loosen the belt and before retightening, the released poison is numbing my leg.

Overhead, large birds circle and even knowin' they're crows, doesn't eliminate the obscene image of vultures flooding my brain.    Another sixty seconds and I suck as much poison out of the wound as I'm likely to get.

This time, even releasing the belt for only ten seconds, I feel my side and left arm go numb.

They'll find me, eventually.    Family'll come lookin' for the alcohol, but they'll find me.

#

Thank God for "hands free" cell phones.  It
allows a woman driver to apply make-up
while texting and still enjoying her
MacDonalds coffee.

#

# 20-FOLLOWING ORDERS

The order had been given:

"Load ammunition and fix bayonets."

My 03-A3 Springfield had long ago proven itself on the 100, 250, 500 and 1000-yard range. It always placed me among the top three in my regiment. I'd been trained for combat. Isn't it funny how those far away from the action call it COMBAT? When you're on the front line, it's just plain fighting and killing and maybe being killed. Yes, I'd been well trained for fighting and I was good at it. I hadn't liked it, but I was good at it. There's always fear when planning for a fight. Once you're in it, there's no more time for fear. You either do what you're trained to do and maybe live or you don't and you probably die.

In lock step, elbow-to-elbow, we move forward.

I'd been in this position before. In the war, I'd killed. I never enjoyed it, but it was necessary and I never felt guilty. I'd always been proud to be a member of the United States Army.

Now, MacArthur says we have to do it and we will, but that doesn't make it right. We're going against unarmed men, American men, ex-soldiers, many of them heroes. But it's 28 July 1932 and we're expected to fight the Bonus Army.

Taking off the safeties on our rifles and carrying with us our shame, we advance.

#

Idaho farmers newly embarked from Southern
California are easily spotted. They still
irrigate their fields from bottled Evion water.

#

97

# 21-BEST METHOD FOR SUICIDE

Zachary had few friends, well very few out of jail and those who were, carried leg-iron monitoring devices and couldn't fraternize with him even if they'd wanted to. He could be a charmer, until caught at something of which he's guilty. That's how he'd worked his way into the lives of Monica and her thirteen-year old daughter, Edith.

Men usually recognized at first meeting that he was morally bankrupt and his soul stained. Though, with his six-foot-six, two hundred forty pound frame, arguments were seldom forthcoming. It was so much easier to just walk away and find another bar. Only women were attracted to him. Bar support was about all he was good for, he'd lost every job he'd ever been coaxed into trying. Other than seducing and living through the largesse of gullible women, his only other talent was fishing.

Monica is normally a good judge of character, but then as P.T. said, there's one born every minute. He was an overnight guest only on the occasions Monica felt low, having heard from or about her ex, Edith's father.
Edith, though, was too young and inexperienced to have developed wariness about men. Zachary was sharp enough to pick up on her extreme vulnerability and as might be suspected, would surely, some day, try to take advantage.

\* \* \* \* \* \*

Memorial Day weekend, all official offices were closed, so a hiker led the police to the body. It was left waiting on a slab for the local consulting coroner to return from his long weekend. The autopsy finally concluded that Zachary had died of natural causes, but the sheriff, after investigation, listed the death as suicide.

* * * * * *

"Sheriff, Jack Evans, Coer 'd Alene Union, a pleasure to meet you.  I'm following the Zachary Clark case and I have to ask why you changed the coroner's report to suicide."

The sheriff eases his oversize bulk into the reclining chair, pulls his boots off and rubs his bunions.  "Why're you interested in this.  Ain't nobody here in Challis high enough on the social ladder to draw you away from the golf tournaments, political rallies and mall openin's."

Jack takes a seat opposite and accepts the offered cup of coffee from the dispatcher.  "I'm always interested in cases that seem to offer more than a three-line obituary."

"That's 'cause you didn't know Zachary.  Had he been found with six gunshot wounds in the back, no one 'round here'ud demand an investigation."  He holds up his hand as Jack starts to respond.  "But just to ease your mind, I'll tell ya.  The scene showed no signs of outside interference and proof that he committed suicide.  The only thing questionable was when did he develop a conscience?  Everybody who knew him accepted the fact that he'd meet his end by a jealous husband.  If that'd happened I doubt we'd even file charges.  See he was quite a ladies man and seldom limited himself to single women."

Jack frowns.  "So, what evidence lead you to the suicide conclusion?"

"Well, he had a secret fishin' spot somewhere on the Salmon.  I don't think anyone else knew its whereabouts. If a hiker hadn't found the body we'd aprobly never missed him.  He'd been dead four days for' we was

99

notified.   Now here's the kicker.   Beside the body was a pile a empty peanut shells."

"How does that qualify as evidence?"

"He died of asphyxiation.   The autopsy showed that his throat swelled up and constricted his airway.   He was allergic to peanuts.   I'm one of the few who knew about the allergy.   We both grew up here and I went to school with the S.O.B."

"So there's no reason to question anything, call for a second autopsy?"

"Kinda hard to do.   He was cremated yesterday. This is a small community and it's less financial burden on the locals to store an urn than to pay fer funeral costs."

* * * * * *

Monica washes dishes as the local radio station announces that the memorial service for Zachary Clark went unattended.   Edith looks up at her mother and puts aside her American History textbook.

"Why, mom?"

"I'm not sure I follow."

"About Zach.   I saw you preparing the sandwiches. You mixed peanut butter with mustard and replaced the mild Anaheim peppers with jalapenos."

"Oh."

"He was sure to eat the peppers first.   After that his taste buds would so deadened he'd never discern the taste of peanuts.   And he was going fishing where no one would hear if he called for help.   What I can't figure is how you knew he was allergic or where his secret fishing spot was."

Monica wipes her hands and takes a seat on the couch beside her daughter   She sets a crystal bowl of shelled peanuts on the coffee table between them.   "The first night he stayed over I offered these and he told me.

100

I knew about his fishing spot because I followed him. I thought his "going fishing story" was just a cover for meeting another woman. I…guess I was jealous."

"But you haven't explained why."

"You knew he was still sleeping on the couch, I hadn't yet given in to his line of seduction. Although, I'm sure he spread rumors about adding me to his conquests. The last time he stayed over, the night before he…, well, anyway, I heard him get up in the middle of the night. He was too young to have prostate problems. So when he entered your room…"

"Oh, but…"

"Yes, you told him to stop, but I heard the hesitancy in your voice. You rejected him <u>that</u> time, but I knew he'd keep trying. I had to protect my only daughter. The law couldn't do anything. I knew he'd pursue you when I wasn't around."

Edith takes her mother's hands in hers. "When you went to see if your plan had worked, I followed you. You'd forgotten the one thing that would lead unquestioningly to a verdict of suicide." She stretches and hugs her mom. "<u>I</u> left that pile of empty peanut shells by the body."

The tears flowing down both their cheeks are not shed for Zachary.

#

You can easily spot a predator because both
eyes are in front of its face.

#

101

# 22-CITY OF ANGELS

*Friday 10:00 P.M.*

It was June, my partner Ed Tucker and I were working the night watch out of Hollywood Division. We'd gotten a call about a jumper. Well, I couldn't expect to forget that Criminals don't quit on weekends and it's my job to make them pay for their disrespect. My name's Thursday and I'm a cop.

We pulled a black and white out of the garage and headed down Sepulveda. The air was so thick you could taste it, if you were dumb enough to want to. It was the kind of night that makes normal people wish they belonged to a gang so they'd have an excuse to smash things and blame it on the environment.

It turns out the "jumper" was face down in half an inch of the Los Angeles River. It couldn't have been any softer than if he'd hit the cement three feet on either side of his all points landing. We roped off an area to search for clues.

We needed to learn who the guy had been before he'd flattened himself with a forty foot jump into "No More Problems Land."

There was a lot of stuff near-by; old clothes, food wrappings and other assorted garbage. Most, if not all of it, belonged to the drifters who call the shade of an overpass home. But this guy was well dressed, had no calluses, a neat haircut and fifty dollar Florshiems that wouldn't have been there if uniforms from the passing patrol car had been ten minutes slower getting down the slope.

While waiting for the black Mariah to come for the body, we took photos. It was clear by the pooling blood

102

that he hadn't been dead more than a few hours. First thing was to I.D. the guy; meanwhile, we'd ask around. His Hart Shaftner & Marx tweed jacket was almost new. There were only six stores in Los Angeles that carried the brand; maybe somebody would recognize him as a customer.

## *Saturday 4:00 P.M.*

We'd worked a double shift and weren't through yet. The fingerprints and photos had turned up a few possibles, but no real hit. The canvass of the men's wear store gave us the name of an Ephram Tandy who fit the general description of our D.B.. The address was a duplex in Topanga Canyon and with a U.S.C.-Stanford football game, the Hollywood Bowl's Liberace concert, the Rose Bowl Flea Market running till dark, I think everybody in southern California was on one of the crowded freeways. Even with red lights and siren it would take over an hour to make the trip, but there was nothing else to do.

The manager, a weaselly little guy obviously still griped at his mother for not giving him the genetic looks of Victor Mature, opened his door a crack.

"Thursday and Tucker, L.A.P.D., we need to see apartment 2a."

He hemmed and hawed, finally reluctantly let us in. It was a typical seventy-five dollar a month place including utilities and pool. Cheap furniture and scant decorations, kept neat and orderly but with few personal belongings. Fridge had the basic staples, all generic brands. He was either cheap or living on a tight budget.

"Hey, Joe, look at this."

I segued from the kitchen into the bedroom. Ed had the closet door open and was fanning the clothes hangers.

103

"He had a limited wardrobe, but everything is top quality."

"Yeah, helped by accessories."

The dresser showed a dozen silk ties, cravats, belts with solid gold buckles, flashy rings and watches, a lot of polo shirts and argyle sox.

"So he was either a gigolo or an aspiring actor."

"Joe, you sayin' you make that two separate classifications?"

I smiled, cause I'm usually the one who gets off the zingers. Our best lead was a candid photo of him at some beach house party. An unrecognizable blonde, her back to the camera, sprawled on a chaise, but in the background, a marker warned surfers about the tides. There wasn't time to completely canvass Malibu, but my friend Jason, on the Coast Guard Beach Patrol might recognize the site. There was no dial tone on the phone here, so we headed back toward the office and on the way we stopped at a gas station.

Ed bought a couple of bottles of Delaware Punch while I dropped a dime in the pay phone and got my friend on the third ring. He wasn't happy, being taken away from a fish fry, but agreed to look at the photo if I'd bring it by. It was only a couple of miles off our course.

Climbing the flagstone steps to his bungalow, we caught the pungent odor of the bar-B-cue grille smoke from the back porch. Jason took a quick look at the photo. We weren't invited to stay.

"Yeah, that's the sign at mile twenty-seven and this is probably the Christa Meader house. She's always having parties there for stars and wanna-bes."

A quick call to stats pulled two addresses for Miss Meader. There was still enough daylight to find our way up Coldwater Canyon to an estate with about six thousand steps from the quarter-acre parking pad up to the front

104

door.    A butler, fresh from a Billy Wilder film, opened the door and acted like we were something he should have wiped off his shoes after a run in the park.

"Los Angeles Police, we're here to talk to Miss Meader."

"I shall see if she is receiving.    If you will be so kind as to wait here."

He shut the door in our faces.    A warrant would have opened it again, but smashing it down with a battering ram would have been faster and more satisfying. He was back in about forty-seconds and allowed us to enter.    The foyer was like a Rajah's palace.    I didn't know anyone who lived like that; don't think I'd ever want to.    The woman floated down the spiral staircase like an Egyptian Queen.    At a distance she was as beautiful as she'd been in all her pictures.    Up close you realized it was a small fortune that kept her looking that way.    She held out her hand.
I wasn't sure if she expected me to kiss it, shake it or both, so I pulled my badge, and avoided the contact.

"Miss Meader, I appreciate you taking time to see us."

I held out the photo, expecting her to take it or at least lean forward for a closer look.

She did neither.

"Can you identify this man and tell us your connection to him?"

"I assume he was at one of my parties.    I have them almost every week-end at my beach house and over the last few months there have been at least a thousand guests I don't know and wouldn't recognize if I ever saw them again."

"You haven't really looked at the picture long enough to tell if this is such a person."

Her eyes flashed and for a moment I could swear she meant to throw the near-by Ming Vase at me. She recovered her aplomb, but spoke through clenched teeth.

"I'm sure that if I <u>have</u> seen him, I've seen a thousand just like him. Hanger's-on, talent-less hacks who think that simply touching my robe will bring them instant stardom."

"So...you're saying you never knew him?"

"I'm saying if I ever knew him I <u>might</u> remember, he'll <u>certainly</u> remember me."

"And you've never heard the name Ephram Tandy?"

"That name rings no bell."

"Well, thanks for your time. We'll find our way out."

Back at headquarters we finally got fingerprint results from central records.

"Joe, we got him. Rupert Manheim. Only had a juvie record in Detroit, been clean out here. Vital Stats show he legally changed his name to Ephram Tandy."

"You got a picture, Ed?"

"Yeah, but it's a little dated."

"Let's take it down to the morgue, see if it matches the body."

Dr. Yancy explained why the photo bore so little relationship to our corpse.

"First off he had cheek implants and a chin tuck to give him the Kirk Douglas dimple. The eyes were helped by colored contacts and he'd had his ears pinned back. I'd say he spent some major coin getting all this work. If it was done around here you should be able to find out who wielded the knife."

"Better still, we might learn how he paid for all that?"

It took us another shift to find the thread we'd been chasing. Juan Beize from Central Division Vice came up with the tie-in.

"Miss Meader has had a series of <u>escorts</u> over the past few years, all considerably younger than she. The last of record was the late Ephram Tandy."

Ed called and said we had more questions for Miss Meader. The butler offered to see if anyone might receive us and left before he could be pinned to the idea that we were coming regardless of the reception. Ed was left holding a dead phone.

When we arrived Miss Meader greeted us almost warmly. She was flanked by her press agent, lawyer, psychiatrist, and studio publicist.

They were seated as if posed by Ansel Adams, lacking only the POOF of black powder flash for the still life. In color it would do justice to a Norman Rockwell-Saturday Evening Post cover.

"We have more questions that need answers, Miss Meader. Why did you lie to us about the man in the photo?"

"Yes, I've had a chance to reflect on that. You see, he never looked like that in life. When I realized it must have been him…Ephram, well, I just couldn't bear to think of him…like that."

"Dead, you mean?" Where were you last night between seven and ten P.M.?"

"Oh, but he wasn't…I mean I was rehearsing lines with my diction coach. Actually we didn't get through until one A.M. Is that all then, detectives?"

"Not exactly.    That's cleared up, now can you account for your whereabouts on Friday evening from six P.M. until three A.M.?"

"Well, yes…we…were, that is, I was on location in Ensenada earlier that week, I returned exhausted Friday afternoon, took sleeping pills and fell into bed."

Her press agent stood, placed a hand conspiratorially on her shoulder and smiled saccharinely at us.

"Surely you're not implying that Miss Meader had anything to do with this?"

I pulled a pair of cuffs from under my coat, glared at him.

"You've used up all your lines and you're not even listed in the cast.    Now I only want to hear from Miss Meader.    Any more dialogue from the rest of you and you'll all sweat out the night on a puke-covered bench in the drunk tank."

It got as quiet as a Master's putting green with Arnie about to sink a seventy-yard double eagle put.

A phone rang distantly and the butler's footsteps rang hollowly from the foyer on the fifty yards of tile floor.    Finally, the ten-foot teak double doors were opened and he announced a call for detective Thursday.  I took it while the others sat as reverently as if the Oscar for Best Actress was about to be named.    I returned and said there was a break in the case and we'd be leaving, but it might be necessary for us to return.    In the car I shared the update with Ed.

"Vice just added the spice our recipe needed.    It seems Mr. Tandy was a regular at several gay bars.    He always came in alone, never left that way."

Ed's eyebrows did a lift-off.

"So, did our Miss Meader know and if so when did she know?"

108

"Exactly.   It makes the cheese more binding."
By midnight we called it quits.

## Monday 9:00 A.M.

The day shift had gathered a shoebox full of data for us.   We sorted the significant material into chronological order.   By noon, after tacos at the "Heart-Burn Ole" stand we headed back to Meader's place.   This time we were let in without the normal fuss.   Miss Meader greeted us with only her attorney in attendance.   I aimed my question directly at her.

"Miss Meader, your alibi doesn't wash, you and your car were seen both on Melrose and where the body of Mr. Tandy was dumped.
Now with your attorney to advise you I will ask you again.   What do you know about the death of this man?

"Man?   He wasn't a MAN, he, he wanted   he was a…"

Her attorney took her elbow.

"Miss Meader, Christa, I must warn you against any more comments."

"Why, they obviously know what he was.   I couldn't let my public learn that he dumped me, ME a major star, idolized by millions, constantly proposed to by men.   That's bad enough, but to be dumped for a…another man.   It just couldn't happen.   I guessed it and followed him to that…place.   I sent in a note, saying I was going to inform the whole world what he was.   He came out and begged me not to.   I said I'd think about it if he came with me.   He was willing to do anything, the creep.   I drove out to the river.   At the overpass I got out to walk, he followed and part way across I convinced him that I'd had a change of heart.    He let his guard down, leaned back against the railing. It was so easy, it just took the slightest push and it was all over."

Newspaper and cameramen are always hanging around the station, so we stopped two blocks short. I took the bracelets off her and let her fix her make up. As we reached the station we let her elegant stride precede us like the movie star she'd once been. This is my town and just like all towns it has a sleazy side but it doesn't always have to be shown that way on the front page.

#

Did you ever wish they gave those Victoria's<br>Secret models some dialogue? Yeah, me<br>neither.

#

# 23-HOW TO SUSTAIN A LASTING AND LOVING RELATIONSHIP WITH A WOMAN

Science has not, as yet, determined the age of the scroll found in recently excavated ruins of ancient Persia. It is believed that this work is part of a library from some wise man of prehistoric times. Possibly a Dr. Phil of the past? The exciting discovery was partially uncovered by military action taken in a recent insurgent uprising in the area.

Expert Anthropologists from Cambridge University and the Royal British Museum have just translated the text and by carbon dating it is expected that within days we may know when, and possibly what civilization, left behind this work for edification of future generations.

Here is the text just as it came from the scrolls of dark and curling parchment:

*"Whenever a woman wants to listen, you talk. When she wants to talk, you listen." End of message.*

Although, she never pays any attention to what you say anyway and the things she wants to talk about are always the same old nonsense,

You promised we could remodel, my mother is coming for a short stay, surely you're not going to wear that, why can't you be more sensitive, I wish you would make new friends, you never take me anyplace, I haven't a thing to wear anyway, does this dress make me look fat?...bla, bla, bla.

#

If your parachute fails to open, most manufacturers suggest that you climb back into the airplane and exchange it for another.

#

## 24-RIGHTING A WRONG

"If those are too tight I can loosen them a bit."

The old man shifted on the oak bench where the marbled hallway's hard surfaces echoed every sound accusingly back at him.

"No, I'm fine. I'm...well, it doesn't really matter, does it?"

He shook his thin wrists and the handcuffs jingled like a ten-cent bell.

The soft voice and friendly young face belied the inherent threat this young man possessed, Noel Crenshaw, the Magic Valley County Prosecuting Attorney. "So, before you're arraigned I must get your statement."

The grey head and lifeless thin blue eyes of the detainee stared at nothingness. Even the early spring ever-new, always old sounds of cooing doves through the recently opened transoms were lost on him.

"You never met my wife, Marilyn. You couldn't have, we lost her so long ago. We met at a Saturday night U.S.O. dance near the end of the war. She'd come with a busload of nurse volunteers to Wendover where I was stationed. I'd been assigned to a B29 group scheduled to leave for the South Pacific island of Tinian. A freak accident from a falling chain hoist broke my arm and they sent me to a hospital in Twin Falls. We met again and it was instant love from then on. Well, the war ended before my arm healed and I took my discharge here. They offered to send me home to Green Meadow, Colorado, but I chose to stay with her. She'd have gone with me, but making her happy meant more to me. She'd grown up here and loved the area. We were married two weeks later, actually, by a municipal judge here in this courthouse."

The occasional click of heels and murmuring of clerks shuffling armloads of redundant papers from one office to another couldn't intrude in the elder's remembrance of a better time.

"With a new job and a new wife, I thought the world could offer me nothing better than what I already had. We were so happy, I needed nothing else, but she wanted--we wanted--to have a child, someone who would be a part of us both. We tried for three years with no results. Then the doctor told us we were to have a gift from heaven. The house was small, one of those five thousand dollar cottages built for returning service men. I'd saved enough to afford an upgrade to a three-bedroom ranch style out on the canyon rim.   I spent every spare minute making one room into a nursery.

Then, in the seventh month, we learned that we had a problem.   The baby had twisted and was cutting off the blood and nourishment supply from the umbilical cord. The threat to the baby was obvious, but Marilyn didn't realize that she was in danger as well.   I rushed her to the hospital on a Saturday night.   She died eight hours later. They took the baby, but gave the child only a forty-percent chance of survival.

I just sat in shock for hours.   Finally, I accepted the fact that my wife was gone, but a part of her remained. The first sight of my daughter was through a thick glass. She was two months premature and blue from an inadequate supply of blood.  They kept her there until the normal delivery time.

The day I took her home, Elizabeth only weighed six pounds, but she had her mother's sparkling eyes and you could see the joy of life in her struggle to be whatever God had meant her to be.   I spent every night for the first six months making her special formula.

As she grew, we did things together.   She couldn't learn enough about everything from fishing for trout in the Snake River, calling bull elk to within feather-throwing distance on Soldier Mountain, snowshoeing across the Owyhee plateau, kayaking down the Salmon River rapids and photographing wild hummingbirds nesting in the South Hills and searching the Hagerman bluffs for mastodon bones.   As a teen-ager she was head cheerleader, debating champion, chess master and science editor of the school paper.

By the time I realized that my life of enjoyable cigarette smoking had caught up with me, I decided to take an early retirement from the Shoshone Falls power plant.

Elizabeth swore she would take care of me for as long as need be.

But I couldn't let her spend the best years of her life looking after an old man. I forced her to choose between an eastern college and a job of fruit packing or fish hatchery work here.

I couldn't hide my pride when I saw her cross the stage for her diploma. She'd graduated in three years from Rutgers and decided to stay on to see about her masters. Then, that Christmas she emailed that she'd be coming home with a surprise. She'd found a boy who made her heart sing and wanted to show him off and get my approval. I know the typical reaction of a father is to not like anyone his only daughter picks, but this boy was the dream of every mother and Elizabeth became envied by her every girlfriend. How could I object?

They were married and Roger took a job with the City Tax Commission and bought a new five-bedroom home on three acres. For the first year they seemed destined to be the perfect couple. By their first anniversary, I saw hints of strife, but Elizabeth assured me that nothing could be further from the truth. There'd been rumors of missing funds in Roger's department and I assumed that might be causing concern. Then I learned she was pregnant and I'd never seen her happier. But a friend told me he'd seen Roger coming from the Planned Parenthood office with brochures in hand. I confronted my lovely daughter and in a tearful admission, she finally admitted that Roger didn't want a sniveling kid ruining his perfect life and if she wouldn't get rid of it, he would."

The offices on every floor surrounding the rotunda were being closed and locked for the weekend. Sheriff deputies going off shift passed, but Noel shook off their looks of askance and offers of help. As the sounds of activity diminished, the old man seemed to get his second

114

wind.   At least, he sat up straighter and his demeanor took on a more self-assured look.

"My daughter had taken a bad fall down the stairs in her home.   Her husband, on a landing above, had unsuccessfully tried to catch her.   The hospital said she'd be all right, but she'd lost the baby and might be unable to have more.   When I heard from one of your own deputies that the accident seemed to be a staged occurrence, I knew what I had to do."

The laptop's jump drive Noel was using to record the statement ran out and as he retracted it, he hesitated.

"I know you refused an attorney, but you should really stop talking now.   I've secured my friend, Harry Turner as your legal counselor.   He will advise you how to continue.   He's shooting the rapids right now, but he'll be back by tonight."

"No, I want to continue.   I went home and got my issued Army .45.   I hadn't used it in fifty years and the grease was stiff, but it seemed to work properly.   When I confronted Roger, he'd been drinking heavily.   He laughed at me, said I should go home and leave the world to the young people who knew how to run things.   When I asked what he'd done, he said, 'Oh that bitch of a daughter of yours thought she'd stick me with a crying brat.   I made sure that wouldn't happen.'"

"I shot him once.   I'd have used more bullets, but I didn't need to.   He was dead at my feet."

Noel pauses, frowns and slides the new jump drive into place.   "So, Mr. MacIntosh, I'll just paraphrase your last statement.   Your son-in-law, in a drunken stupor, came at you in an unprovoked attack and the gun you'd been cleaning went off.   I can well imagine your anguish at seeing him obscenely sprawled on the floor, victim of a horrid and unpreventable accident.   I'm going to have

Doctor Weiss give you a sedative until you're more lucid."

#

No, darling, I was singing a Gershwin tune; I
wasn't saying, "I love you, porky."

#

# 25-NON-RECIPROCITY

"Mom, he's a stone fox."   Gina and her mother Travis watch as Evan, the high school football coach/English Lit Instructor, throws one muscular leg over the saddle of his Harley Big Boy.   He turns the ignition key and kicks the fiery monster into life.   They try not to stare, but as he fits a crash helmet over his curly, blond, Greek god-like head, they both sigh in unison.   The motorcycle fishtails out onto the now-empty street and Gina pulls her mother toward their eight-year old Toyota and continues her "let's find mom a boyfriend" campaign.

"The school Pep Club try-outs for new cheerleaders are Friday and he'll be there.   He supports all athletic related events."

"But I have to get the estimates ready for the new highway bond issue…"

"Yes, mother, but you don't have to do it on the weekend and it's the one place you could run into him naturally.   If it doesn't happen there, I'll have to arrange something more obvious."

"I'm not going to…"

"I know, mom.   We've been through this a thousand times.   You don't need a man, you're complete and your life is fully rewarded just as things are.   Must we go through this litany every time?   The difference is,

116

you want companionship, adult conversation, comfort, and your mind to be challenged. You want someone to empathize with you, to cry when you're sad, laugh when you're glad."

"Yes, but that doesn't mean…"

"That you're going to settle for just anybody? Don't I know that? Haven't I been through other possibles? Evan, Mr. Dayton, is by far better than all the rest and you are not going to let him slip away, mom. Do you hear me?"

Silence for response. Then,

"What does "stone fox" mean?"

"Means if you don't grab him some woman with a better grip on reality will snatch him up."

"It isn't as if I can't…"

"Mom, you haven't had a real date in like five years. So don't even try that…I'm doing fine routine on me."

"But you said he's…"

"Twenty-nine. And you're thirty-one. But thirty is the new twenty. Now doesn't that make it sing for you?"

"Oh, I don't know, Gina."

She hangs back as her daughter pushes her into the driver's seat and comes around to sit beside her and continue her filibuster. The car starts toward the Perrine Bridge and as they cross the Snake River, Gina has an inspiration.

"Dad called." Silence. "His condo has an extra bedroom." Silence "He says I'm welcome anytime." Silence "For as long as I want."

Gina adds more pressure. "He asked if I'd given any more thought to finishing high school in Denver."

Travis tries to squeeze away a tear and turns her head, hoping Gina hasn't seen it.

* * * * * *

"Now this isn't a real date. I just said I'd meet him after the Pep Rally for coffee."

"Yes, mother."

Gina tries to keep her happily shining eyes from exposing her excitement. She has limited success. When her mother comes from the bathroom looking—she thinks—her best, Gina manages, just barely, to hide her disappointment.

"How do I look?"

"Great, mom. There's just a few things. Let's get you some bi-focals, pull your amazing mane of strawberry-blonde hair—hair that every other woman in town would give their last dollar for—into a tight bun. Then we'll lengthen the dress till it covers your ankles. You'll look just like Ms Tanager, the school librarian. She hasn't had a date in like…forever."

"I don't think roasting your mother is the proper attitude for a thirteen-year-old."

"'Most fourteen and are you serious? He's not interested in developing a "Mother/son Relationship."

"That's enough, young lady. I think I've…"

Gina jumps and hugs her mother. They cry together as they sway back and forth.

"I just don't want to look a fool."

"Mom, you worked you way through Brown for your Accounting degree, then got your masters at Colorado. You're amazing and if he can't see that right off, then he's a loser. But you got to know that men are vision oriented. They need a picture they can hold on to."

"Are you sure you're not the mother and I'm the daughter?"

"Sometimes I wonder. But now let's get you into your black cocktail dress, heels and black hose. And braid you hair in a French twist."

118

* * * * * *

Gina and her girlfriends gather nervously before the cheerleader try-outs. Several times she's asked, "Isn't that your mom up there in the stands, the one drawing stares from all the guys?"

Gina manages each time to divert their attention to routines they've not perfected.

* * * * * *

The first home game of the season and the Bruins are favored to win over the Hailey Comets by three points. The Hailey team arrives in private limos. Their custom tailored jerseys come from Abercrombie and Fitch. Their Helmets, designed by Eddie Bauer, are delivered by special messenger to each individual player. It's rumored that their school uses specially bottled Evian to water their Ernest Hemmingway Field.

The Twin Falls team wears three-year old hand-me-down uniforms that each player must launder at home. This is Mr. Dayton's first year coaching. He's not had the faculty support he'd been promised and his starting defensive line is composed of undersized freshmen and sophomores. His starting quarterback, Jimmy Bartlett, is good, but maybe only sixty per-cent as good as he thinks he is and the wide receivers all suffer from dropitis.

Looking to the sideline where all the young hopefuls are seated, he sees Gina. She smiles and the angels sing. He seems to draw strength from it, and searching the disappointingly thin crowd, he spots Travis.

He takes one look at her, that's all he meant to do, and then his heart stands still.

* * * * * *

At the end of the regular season the Bruins are eight and three. Not enough to garner the championship, but good enough to bring an encouraging mood to the faculty, trustees and Bruin Boosters. They're already making plans for the next season. More than a dozen fundraisers promise to enlarge and improve the stadium. The Magic Valley Ford Dealership has pledged a new team bus, feasibility studies are being made for an electronic scoreboard and the fathers of the players have sponsored a high-tech radio link and public address system. Evan and Travis are a regular couple, and although no public announcement of engagement has been made, it's a small town and what happens isn't nearly as important as what is perceived to be happening.

Gina has her eye on Jimmy. Although steadily improving, he still believes he's the best thing since sliced bread. His teammates have, half in jest-half in earnest, presented him with a four-foot wide hat makers' display model. It takes two players to present him with the size 96 gift. Gina intends to change him, but at present she hasn't developed physically enough to be noticed by him. At every opportunity, her mother tries to dissuade her from putting her current social life on hold in anticipation of a questionable future. The now, fourteen-year old smiles and patronizingly pats her mother on the arm.

"Travis, based on your limited experience do you really want to give me 'matter-of-the heart' advice?"

Travis is smart enough to know when not to respond.

It's best to start with grapes or raisins when attempting to sneak your nutritious snack into a movie theater.  Wait until you become more proficient before trying watermelon.

# 26-NOT EVERYTHING THAT HAPPENS IN VEGAS STAYS IN VEGAS

*Monday, 8:00 A.M.*

I swagger into the Ground Round and searching the crowd, quickly see my target.  He's sitting with a group of working cowboys and looks almost like one.  I'm wearing the classic uniform of a casino dealer, white blouse, tight black skirt and patent-leather heels.

"Hey you, faux cowboy, I want to talk to you."

Six men turn, in answer to my challenge.  Mitch doesn't.

I walk up and poke him on the shoulder with a stiff index finger.  "You, I'm talking to you."

Finally he gives me the same evaluation that every other male in the place has already made.  On a scale of one to ten, I hope I score at least a seventeen.  (I'd been told that normally, after three in the afternoon, the cigarette smoke will make seeing anything in here a problem, but it's morning. and early, this is not a bar, but the purveyor of the best biscuits and gravy in town.)  It's hard to tell what Mitch's appraisal of me might be, (he's said to be a very good poker player.  His eyes and facial expressions seldom if ever have betrayed his thoughts).

With the toe of his left expensive cowboy boot, he kicks out the only un-occupied chair at his table.

"Please join us. We're honored by your presence."

The others at his table push back their chairs and move to a far corner table. Without a single wasted motion, I lower myself onto the offered chair. My wrap-around dark sunglasses make it impossible for anyone to read my eyes.

"You've been dating my sister for a week. You were out with her last night. She didn't come home and I want to know what you did with her."

"How old is your sister?"

"Twenty-two, what's that got to…?"

"Then it's her business to tell you what she does and who she does it with."

"If you think…"

"What's her name?"

"Tina, but you know that already."

"I don't know any Tina's under the age of ninety-four."

"You fit the description. Where were you between ten last night and seven this morning?"

His gaze, already having taken in my most visible physical attributes, narrows on my face. "I assume you both deal at the Golden Spike?"

"Yes."

"And she's your sister by blood?"

"Of course."

"Then it's clear, you're lying."

I inhale a little too deeply before responding."

"I don't know what you mean."

You're probably a cop and you want my alibi for last night.

122

So, what nefarious deed occurred last night in the great metropolis of Elko, Nevada that you'd want to question me about?"

"You're crazy."

"If you were local, you'd know better." Mitch sips his coffee without losing eye contact with this enigma sitting beside him. "You're Latina. The Golden Spike doesn't hire any Latinas out on the casino floor. The Cowboy Poet Society holds their annual contest at the Golden Spike and last year Mexicans won the top three places. It's politically incorrect and profiling, but since then most locals wouldn't sit where a Latina deals."

Although the patrons continue their breakfasts, they make no noise doing so. It's obvious that no one wants to miss any of our quietly spoken dialogue. Other than regular barroom brawls, this is probably the most excitement since their last P.R.C.A rodeo.

Two men, in the back of a darkened van, both pull off headphones. Their tape recorder and radio receiver continue to operate. "She's been made."

"Yeah, I had no faith in her plan, but she's the hot shot detective from Vegas."

I jerk off my sunglasses with more passion than I should. My natural burnished bronze complexion is now highlighted by a rosy flush.

He knows he's struck pay dirt. "You needn't be angry just because I've outed you. You're undercover, and while I'd love to get you under the covers, I'll answer your questions if you just tell me why."

The surveillance team enters. Their suits and anxiousness mark them as outsiders. They spread, but with Mitch, facing the escape path, they're unable to make a stealthy approach.

They address me. "Maybe this worked in the past, but we told you it wasn't likely to work here, Miss Valez."

"Let's take him to the station, get answers the old fashioned way."

Mitch frowns up at the two. "You're neither old enough to know about old fashioned ways or smart enough to use them."

I express enough attitude toward the two to curl the back hair on a fat man in a speedo caught leering at teenyboppers. "I'll say when we change interview tactics. Now get back to your stations. When I want your help, I'll send for you."

Mitch grins at me. "You have to be more selective when agreeing to baby sit kids."

I turn to Mitch. "Okay, so where were you last night?"

"Hum, I seem to disremember."

"What did you do, and can anybody vouch for your actions?"

"I must have been drinking, 'cause wherever I was and whatever I did, my memory banks are empty. Maybe if you told me why you want to know you'd jog them into place."

"Okay, this is not going the way I want."

I show him my Lieutenant's Nevada Gaming Commission badge.

"I need to talk to your brother, I have an embezzlement arrest warrant for him."

Mitch stands, moves to a corner and calls Neal.

"Don't tell me where you are, but I have some information to impart."

Back at the table, "Neal says he has no knowledge of any embezzlement."

124

"Look, I can wrap this up quickly, if he comes in and answers the charge."

"Yeah, I'm sure he'll jump at the opportunity to put his head in a noose."

"If I fly you to Vegas and show you the evidence, will you convince him that surrendering is his best chance?"

"Sure, and will the kids you're babysitting go too?"

"Yes, they're fully qualified to…"

"Okay, I'll go anyway. Even if we can't be alone, maybe while they're napping we'll spend some intimate time together."

*Monday, 10:33 A.M.*

At the Nevada Gaming Commission Office, Mitch peruses my evidence of an embezzlement of some twelve million from seven casinos.

"How could this happen, if casino security is so good?"

"He had to steal the password and have the proper I.D. to tap into the system at home."

"So if he didn't do it on site, did he just walk out with the data?"

"No, but we found a framed photograph of his wife, Martha, on the wall behind his desk. Built in was a wireless receiver."

"So he just took the thing apart every night before he left?"

"No, coded data can't be copied directly and the building is shielded, to prevent wireless transmissions. We've not found his mobile receiver that accepts the download from the picture frame yet."

"Have you searched his apartment?"

125

"We've had it under surveillance until I can get a warrant."

"I have a key and prior access."

"You'll help me convict your brother?"

"No, but I'll help you clear him of these charges."

At the apartment, we find blood and signs of a struggle.   I put out an all points bulletin to police, state and federal authorities for Martha.

Mitch calls Neal again.   "When did you last see Martha?"

"Four days ago, just before I left for the northern casinos.  Why, is something wrong?   Is she hurt?"

I cover the mouthpiece and whisper:   "If you tell him this is now a possible homicide investigation I'll have to arrest you as obstructing a police investigation."

He tells Neal he'll have to call back and hangs up.

I get a call from LVPD.   They've found Neal's green Wagoneer in the airport long-term parking lot, it's towed to impound.

I frown.   "We'd already determined that neither he nor Martha purchased airline tickets, took a private plane, nor hired a charter flight."

Mitch has some questions of his own.   "How was the embezzlement uncovered?   How old is blood in the apartment?   Is it Martha's blood type?   When was the car left at the airport?   If Neal killed Martha, why take her to the airport?   And if he did, how did he get from the airport?   Why leave his car there?"

He sees a Topaz tie tack atop Neal's dresser. "Martha gave this to him.   He always wore it with a suit while he was working.   He's on vacation now."

The U.S. Border Patrol sends me a fax.   They've found a truck with current Nevada plates abandoned at Mexican border.   The keys are still in the ignition.   It's registered to Mr. Amos Pierce, Henderson, Nevada.

126

Mitch and I drive to Henderson and interview Mr. Pierce. He sold the truck to a man three days ago, didn't bother to follow-up on the re-registration. I show him a photo of Neal.

"Nope, it warn't him."

I ask the Mexican authorities to look for tracks leading south across the border.

"You mean from the Estado Unidos into Mexico?"

"Yes, si."

Mexican authorities find the body of a dead man in a direct line leading south from the truck. They send me a fax photo of the man, Frank Knox.

Mitch and I return to Henderson, show the photo of the dead man to Mr. Pierce.

"Yep, he's the one bought my truck two days ago." He sees, below the photo of dead man, the same photo of Neal, and beneath that, the photo of Martha that he hadn't been shown earlier.

"And that's woman drove him here to get my truck."

"You're sure?"

"Yeah. I'm old, but I ain't senile. Not yet, anyways. She was in a green Wagoneer. Say, does this mean I'll get my truck back?"

I look hard at Mitch. "Two days ago. The blood from the apartment is three days old. So she faked her own death."

I ask the Mexican authorities to search for Martha.

Mitch pulls me out of my chair. "Neal always said that Martha hated hot weather. She'd never leave the apartment in summer. Even between an air-conditioned car and building, the Vegas evenings were too hot for her."

Mitch calls Neal again. Comes back again to explain to me. "Neal says that's why he's waiting in

Canada for her. She wanted a 2^nd honeymoon up here in Banff. She's supposed to be attending a birthday party for her mother in McCall, Idaho. She was to meet him in Canada."

"So if she set this whole thing up, she wouldn't have left without the casino money."

"And the only sure way is if <u>she's</u> the one who embezzled the money." I finger the tie tack. "Maybe this is the receiver that downloaded the data."

"But if Neal had been behind the scam, he wouldn't have left this behind."

"So she used this Frank to buy the truck, leaving no trace to herself?"

"Then she killed Frank to keep all the money for herself and leave no live witness."

"It's all supposition that she stole the money. We don't know if or how she did it."

"You have a better answer?

"No."

Mexican authorities find Martha at The El Mirador in Cabo. They open her security drawer in the hotel vault and find the missing 12 million dollars.

### *Monday 3:27 P.M.*

Mitch grins. "We'll have to go to Cabo."

"What do you mean <u>we</u>, white man?"

"I have to see the money returned to clear Neal. And alone, you may just decide to stay there and live off the money."

"Would that be so bad?"

"Not if we were together."

"I'm going there to extradite your sister-in-law."

"No, my sister-in-outlaw. Book us on a flight. I'll make the hotel reservation."

The Cabo shuttle bus takes us to the El Mirador. Mitch leaves the registration desk carrying only one key.

In the hotel suite, he stands as close as possible. "We can't pick her up from the local gendarmeries until Friday.  That gives us three days to become better acquainted."

His hand finishes unbuttoning my blouse as his words end.

"I know all about you I need to know.  You're a letch."

The soft rustle of my blouse sliding to the floor ends with my words.

"Without me, you may never get back into the States."

The sound of the unzipping of my skirt fills the temporary silence.

"I have my credentials."

"I could say that you're a coyote, smuggling me across the border."

My skirt falls to the floor.

"You're just being silly.  What would that accomplish"

"It would keep us here.  We'd <u>have</u> to get by on that money."

\* \* \* \* \* \*

Room service leaves two breakfasts at the door.  I serve them to the room's only king size bed and without making eye contact with Mitch I throw out:  "This was just a fling, you know.  It means nothing."

"So, with no plan to make this long term, you took advantage of my unsuspecting and naive nature? You would use me and kick me to the curb?"

"No, but I live in Vegas and you have your commodities trading business in Elko. It would never work."

"My business is wherever I plug in my computer. I guess if Cabo and the money is out, I could take Vegas on the measly six figures I make."

#

I've always preferred casual to dress shirts and
ties. It's a throwback to my upbringing. I
come from a long line of horse thieves and I
don't like anything tight around my neck.

#

# 27-REDEMPTION

## *Central Police Station-Morning*

"You're going to ask her to help us? You're kidding, right, Cap.? That'll be a bigger crossover than George Michaels going back in the closet and coming out straight."

"The Lieutenant is right, sir. I mean she's been arrested twenty times."

"Thank you for that update, guys. Have you read the arrest results? No convictions, as in zero, zip, nada, none, etc. Ask her politely to join me for a little operation I think will interest her. Bring her in the side door after shift change. I don't want anyone who might recognize her getting the wrong ideas."

Lieutenant Erskin can't resist expressing his thoughts.

"But, Captain Morgan, the last case only closed 'cause she ran over her partner with the get away car while he was holding all the evidence."

"And how did that end, Sergeant? He was convicted, said she had nothing to do with the deal. He even refused to charge her with running over him, said she'd slid on an icy Logan road."

"But the first time isn't even in her file, 'cause she was eight and she'd conned her boyfriend into sending a note demanding money or they'd kidnap this teacher that had given her a bad time. They got caught because the boy spelled ransom, 'rantzom.' She's always found some dummy so crazy about her he'd do anything she asked."

## Central Police Station-Morning

"She's been in your office quite a while, Cap. She come in without a fuss. Like as if she'd finally met her match and came in to confess all her sins."

"Yeah. I haven't met her yet, have you, Lieutenant?"

"No, sir, don't want to. I choose not to die the victim of a predatory female. I've heard her defined as both a black widow spider and a Venus Fly Trap personified.

Matt moves quickly up the corridor, pushes open the glass door marked--M. Morgan-Captain SLCPD-Bunco Division--and enters his office. Even viewed from behind, she's impressive. Posed atop a corner of his desk, she doesn't bother turning at the sound. He's forced to pick his way around chairs and a credenza covered with stacks of case files not piled as neatly as he'd left them. Behind his desk he ignores his comfortable padded swivel chair. Instead, he stands and looks down at her. It takes a while. There's much to be seen. From the massive swirl of strawberry blonde hair to the wide green eyes, perfect creamy complexion and hourglass body topped by an impressive cleavage, the short, tight, floral green, black and white dress does little to hide any of these attributes. She swings long legs encased in high leather boots. He wraps his hand around one ankle and runs his hand slowly up her calf. She doesn't respond. His hand slides up to her inner thigh. Still no respond. His hand moves higher. Her voice is like warm honey. "If you make it to the Y, you'd best have an engraved golden invitation."

He sits down and smiles up at her.

"I'd heard you don't rattle easily, now I can personally attest that it's true."

*Damn, he's yummy looking, but he can't get me heated up like that and then just quit. Nothing I learned about him mentioned any intimate details.*

"We've never met, Captain. My name is Camellia Baker; my friends call me Cam. You wanted to meet? It can't be anything in my packet and I've gone through all your current cases. None of them relate to me."

"Yes, Miss Baker, I'd..."

"Cam, certainly after all we've been through together."

"Uh...Cam, I'd like your help. This guy Petrosha is bleeding locals of all their savings."

"And why, pray tell would I want to do that?"

"Once you hear the details, I think you'll agree that he needs to be shut down."

*I shouldn't look directly at him. Damn, he's as gorgeous as that guy played Superman on Lois and Clark.*

132

The light is subdued in this quiet, intimate cocktail lounge, the soft vintage music of classic Sinatra ballads and candlelit tables create the proper seduction scene. The drinks are served in footed goblets slightly smaller than a soccer ball, the waiters are discrete and the booths discourage invasive attention.   Cam leans over the tiny table toward Matt.   She downs her full glass and sets it aside.   The view now pays homage to her décolletage.

"So this slezeball is a cancer on society.   Why am I the one to help put him away?"

Her foot comes to rest intimately, as if by accident, against his calf muscle.

"Are you kidding?   You're the queen of scam. Who better to ferret out a bunco artist?"

"You mean 'set a thief to catch a thief.'"

"That's a crude way to put it."

"But accurate.   It's okay; I'm not thin skinned.   But why would you need help?   Your arrest record rivals Elliot Ness."

"How do you know that?"

"I research potential enemies, it's the only way to keep my crown."

"I won't assume anything.   I hope you'll help, but I'll respect your decision either way."

*She's gotta, she's gotta, she's gotta, she's gotta, she--s gotta.*

"It's an intriguing idea, but what's in it for me?"

"Some day you'll meet someone you want to spend your life with and it may be necessary to disclose your past.   I can help scour your record."

"How can you do that?"

"I have my ways."

133

## *White Cornice Apartments-Monday Early Evening*

Cam, holding a small overnight bag, rings the bell of the high-rise.   Matt, with a wet dishtowel and raised eyebrows, opens the door.

"I can't work out of my own home, it's too high profile.   I hoped I could crash here for a couple of days You know, just until I can establish a cover identity."

She slides past so closely that various parts of their bodies make contact

*Oh, she can't do that.*

## *Central Police Station-Morning*

Lt. Erskin hands Matt coffee.   "You sent her out without supervision or back-up?"

"Too risky.   Surely he'll watch his back trail.   I hope it works.   It's my career if it doesn't."

A thick, open file lists the various scams she's known to have worked, but never convicted of.

## *Central Police Station-Three Weeks Later*

The Chief of Detectives calls a meeting.      In attendance are Matt and Lt. Erskin.

"Captain Morgan, I want to discuss your squad's closing of the ponze case."

"Well, sir.   We got help from an undercover source. She managed to learn where he buried his money and how he prospected and recruited new victims.

"Who is this U.A.?   Have we used her before?"

"No, sir.   I think she's worked for N.H.S., her code name is Rachael."

134

## White Cornice Apartments-Early Morning

Matt enters the living room from his bedroom and opens the drapes. On the seven-foot suede couch, Cam looks as tiny as a child. That's if you don't look closely. She's wearing a very flimsy, almost transparent nightgown. He studiously avoids looking closely. She's kicked off the blanket and is semi-wrapped in the sheet.

Matt is setting breakfast on the table when she comes flushed from the shower draped with a large bath towel. She pulls Matt's head down and gives him a kiss much longer and more intimate than might be expected of a thank you for some favor casually requested and easily given. Pouting, then reacting to his latest news.

"You're kidding. Now you say I have to tell these people I'm sorry they were so gullible that I was able to point out their flaws for them?"

"No, you apologize for having scammed them out of their money."

"I thought you'd just make a few keystrokes and zap my record clean."

"I will, after you've made the proper amends."

"Now I know you're crazy? You expect me to give back the money I worked so hard for besides swallowing my pride? Well, I won't do it. You can just go and…and…"

## White Cornice Apartments-Early Evening

Matt carries groceries into his apartment and sees Cam coming from his bedroom wearing only one of his dress shirts, slightly open in front.

"Okay, what's the proper attire for eating crow?"

*Oh, she can't do this to me. I can only take so many cold showers.*

135

Matt smiles inwardly. "That closes the Ormsby Case, now the next…"

"What next? I thought once I did this we were done."

"And we almost are, there are only nineteen more to go."

"No way."

"You want your arrest records expunged and you agreed to do this."

"Under extortionary conditions, but,…but, I'll have no money left."

"You're resourceful, you'll do just fine legally on your wits."

"Stupid agreement!"

*White Cornice Apartments-Early Evening*

Matt enters, his snow boots have failed to keep the knee-high snow from soaking his pants. Cam, seated seductively on his living room couch, is holding a full Martini glass. On the coffee table beside her is a frosted shaker and another glass.

His frown, meant to express dismay; never rises to that level of acceptance.

"Why are you still here?"

"I've had the heat and water turned back on, but it'll take a day to warm up. I didn't think you'd mind my spending another night on your couch."

"How'd you get in?"

"Oh, you really think I need a key?"

She fills the other glass, hands it to him and pats the couch beside her.

136

## White Cornice Apartments-Morning

Matt taps a manila folder with an index finger.

"Now this next one..."

"You're kidding. That would eat up the last of my nest egg and I'm too young for Social Security."

He makes no response, simply waits for her to finish her tirade.

"There are no words to express how much I detest and despise you."

## White Cornice Apartments-Afternoon

"But this last one is not, you can't, I mean there's no one to apologize to."

"You convinced Mrs. Potter that you were her long lost heir, got her to turn over her estate to you before it was too late. You could have waited, she only lasted another two months."

"But after all the back taxes, it was only a hundred and fifty thousand and there's nobody left to return it to."

"That's why I've arranged for you to make an endowment for that amount, in her name, to the "Little Sisters of the Poor Orphanage.""

"That...that's where I..."

"Grew up, that's why it goes full cycle. It ends the old and starts the new."

"How did you learn that? Those records are supposed to be sealed."

"It was easy, Rachael. You were the only Hebrew named child in their charge. I'm Catholic, I know all the Nuns there. As a boy I shoveled their walks. And our winters are long."

She visibly struggles with this new and complex concept.

*Well, that answers a question I didn't want to ask, but it paves no yellow brick road for me.*

"Why did you choose to operate here anyway? I think Chicago, Los Angeles, Seattle or Denver would be more lucrative."

"I tried other cities, but people here are the easiest to scam."

## *White Cornice Apartments-Late Evening*

Matt wakes to find his covers thrown off and Cam sitting on the bed beside him. She's wearing the same outfit as when they first met.

She stares down at him and with weak and tremulous words (not at all her "Look out world, here I come" voice). "I didn't want to leave without saying goodbye."

"What? Why? You don't need to leave."

*I can't tell him. He'd laugh. Why couldn't he be ugly, or stupid, or…well anybody else?*

"I just have to go."

"But nobody will take care of your beautiful house the way it deserves."

"I've listed it for sale."

"Why?"

"Well, there's reasons why I have to leave."

"What?"

"I can't face the possibility of running into you."

"That makes it extremely difficult on me.. How can I propose to you if I don't know where you are?"

"What? You couldn't marry me, after what I've been…"

138

"Not the girl you were, but I'm marrying the woman you've become."

He pulls her down prone beside him.

She tries to twist away, but he catches her in a kiss each time she comes full front.  She struggles, but inefficiently.

"I can't believe you could forget my past."

"What past?  Your file mentions you were questioned a few times.  I assume you were a witness, helping the D.A. close a few cases."

"How would you introduce me to your friends? This is a poor little gutter snipe I tried to make into a semi-presentable person?"

"No, I'd just say I'd like you to meet my wife, Cam."

#
There will always be those around who
haven't done it, to tell those who have done it,
how they should have done it.
#

# 28-TAKE ADVANTAGE OF YOUR COMMUNITY SERVICES

The silence is deafening, even more so here where the place was built for silence and the street sounds are non-existent at three A.M. Then...the sound of shallow breathing, another, and another. In the light from the outside streetlight, three ski-masked figures all in black crouch and duck-waddle toward the Idaho Room.

"BUMP, JIGGLE, GASP."

"Sh..."

"I didn't..."

"Sh..."

"It wasn't me, I..."

"Shut up, you idiot."

The TICK of metal lightly scraping metal.

"Are we in?"

"Sh..."

"No."

"Let me try the knob."

"Sh..."

"You jerk, this is the most secure section of the entire place. You think they went home and left the door unlocked."

BUMP, JIGGLE.

"I can't seem to..."

"Push, don't pull you moron."

"Okay, we're in. Quit pushing, LENA."

"I told you no names."

"What, you think they set up a recording device just to hear us give our names as we rob the place?"

"Come on, let's..."

"Hey, there's a lot more here than I expected. How do we know what to take?"

"We'll just have to take it all."

"Damn, you shudda gotten a list."

"How we gonna carry all this?"

"You'll have to take it in shifts."

"Yeah, and like we take the first shift while you do your nails or go out for coffee?"

"No, I'll help carry the small, delicate stuff."

"Hey, there's a cart out in the hall. We can load that up."

"Good idea." They load the cart and it fishtails down the hall. "SQUEEK, SQUEEK. The cart has one recalcitrant wheel and three with dry axles.

"OKAY dumb ass. How do we get this down the stairs?"

"We don't have to. We use the elevator. You think I spent those three years in the seventh grade for nothing?"

DING.

"Sh…"

"Get it inside and push the button."

NOISY ELEVATOR MOVEMENT.

"Hey, this is the basement."

"The stupid thing doesn't stop at the main floor."

"I didn't know."

"You boob, now we have to carry all this stuff UP one flight. That's harder than carrying it down."

"Yeah, and…"

"Stop bickering and get it upstairs. I'll bring the car. Cops make their rounds pretty soon and they like to sit across the street and eat donuts in the park."

"We shoulda brought boxes..."

Three dark figures stumble under heavy loads. The car dome light has been removed. At least they did that right. Finally the entire contents are loaded into the vintage Toyota station wagon in the Twin Falls Public

Library lot.   It starts with a complaint, but makes it onto Fourth Ave East, turns left and heads toward Kimberly just as a black and white parks across the street with a box of donuts and…well, you know what I mean.

Twenty minutes later, with the car unloaded and the three huddled in the dark, unfurnished, unheated cottage, their ski masks are removed.   Lena opens a bottle of champagne, the two hold glasses at the ready.   The cork pops, the bottle is upended and…nothing.   The wine is frozen solid.   In impotent fury, the two men sit uncomfortably, shivering, knees knocking.

"Okay, it's not the celebration we expected, but by tomorrow we'll be rich and drinking while somebody else pours."   Lena pulls the black sweater over her head. Underneath, she's wearing an orange turtleneck.   Even in black, her figure is impressive, but in the thin sweater, she's an orange grower's fantasy.   What with…well, you know what I mean.

"You two get some sleep.   I'll make contact first thing in the morning.   We'll pick up the money and be out of here by noon.   The stuff's safe in the shed, as long as it doesn't rain."

The departing Toyota leaves the men in the dank, depressing gloom, too cold to sleep, lips shivering too much to hold a cigarette.

"I can barely concentrate on the visual of enjoying the lights of the Vegas strip.   The showgirls, gambling, booze, showgirls, fancy cars, showgirls, gambling, booze, and…well, you know what I mean."

"Quit hogging the blanket, numb nuts, my face is freezing."

"Your FACE?   I can't even feel my ass."

"Your ass is nothing to brag about, I can't figure why anyone'd want to feel it."

Eight A.M., nine A.M., ten A.M., still no word from Lena.

"You think she took the stuff and skipped out on us?"

"WE'VE got the stuff, dumb ass."

"Oh, yeah."

"Besides, she's your sister. Would she do this to you?"

"Well, she used to tease me when we were kids."

"Why, just cause you used to put your shoes on the wrong feet?"

"Only till I was twelve."

\* \* \* \* \* \*

The SOUND of the Toyota returning stops this trip down memory lane. Lena opens the hatchback and motions to them to hurry.

"Get the stuff loaded."

"I thought they was gonna pick it up…"

"Plan's been changed."

"But how are we…"

"I'll tell you on the way."

"Aren't you going to help us load?"

"These are twenty dollar heels and the ground there is muddy. I'll keep the car warm."

With the car loaded and fishtailing out the muddy driveway, she explains.

"Our buyer only wanted the first editions and original papers from the Lewis and Clark Exhibit. He said we grabbed the original peace treaty and other rare historical documents and articles and now all the stuff is too hot to handle."

"I knew all that Next Pierce stuff wasn't right."

"Nez Perce, not next pierce, you numb nut."

143

"Anyway, I tried a few other private collectors, same story, but it's not a complete loss. The insurance company said…"

The car is heading west on Fourth Avenue when the men spot three city-police cars parked nose to tail on one side of the street.

"…that if we…"

On this side of the street four sheriff's cars line the curb.

"…would put…"

The car turns into the Library's parking lot. Across the street are twelve emblazoned state trooper squad cars; a few more are probably undercover vehicles.

"…all the stuff back, exactly as we found it they wouldn't press charges."

She gives them a disarming smile and gets out of the car. Ninety-six eyes watch as she turns full profile.

"They even agreed to pay us regular library wages while we're doing it. We only have to dust everything as we go."

Numb Nuts and Dumb Ass look like eight year olds who've wet their pants. No, more like thirty year olds who've wet their pants. Frankly, it's not clear they haven't.

"The place is…"

"…Crawlin' with cops."

"That's just to guarantee we have a clear path and are not hampered doing it."

It only takes four hours to complete the task. And when they finish, they each receive, after all deductions, a check for $35.10. Quite a step up, since dividing by all the hours they spent planning and executing the heist, they each netted fifty-seven cents an hour and that's more than they'd have made working in the prison laundry. That and a full tank of gas won't get them to Vegas, but they might make it to Jackpot.    Maybe there's actually something to the phrase that "Crime doesn't pay."

#

Eagles didn't evolve from fish and man didn't
evolve from a monkey.  It's only his behavior
that leads to that conclusion.

#

## 29-JINGLE BELLS

He sat there as in a daze.   His feet ached from the hunched position he'd been in for so long; he didn't know how long.    Didn't even realize his arms were cramped. He seldom felt such things.   He was confused; his head always ached when these things happened.   The derelict apartment had no heat or lights.   Occasionally from the street an errant headlight illuminated the foul messages he'd splattered on the walls.   He wouldn't read them-- didn't understand their meaning.   He couldn't remember why he did these things.    Subliminally he heard, but didn't respond to the cheery sounds from passing last minute Christmas shoppers.

Time to get on with the business at hand.    He straightened from the animal-like crouch he'd been in. Then...from the broken street window on a chilling breeze wafted the soft tinkle of the Salvation Army kettle-man's bell, and he was back in the basement furnace-room where the man always took him.   Five years old, he was too scared to cry out.

The tinkle of his mother's Christmas ribbon and bell lapel-piece came back to him and brought a false feeling of safety.

As he pulled the plank buttressed against the shattered door and they squeezed through the narrow gap, past the littered opening, he lessened his grip on the terrified six year old; the rag held over her mouth had slipped away. The bells again, more pain, he didn't want to do this any more, hadn't ever wanted to do it. He let the girl go and with her escape, he looked down at the razor sharp knife in his hand.

Without pause, he sliced it across his jugular and the blood that poured out covered his hands. He knew it was the only way they'd ever be cleansed.

#

Men have trouble interfacing with women
because they expect logic somehow is
involved. Women have trouble responding to
conversation with a man because they assume
that intelligence is a common trait.

#

# 30-REVENGE IS A DISH BEST SERVED HOT

Climbing astride tired horses and leading a fresh mount, two grinning men send clods of rich, tillable soil airborne as demanding more speed, they rake spurs across already bloody flanks. From nearby bushes, moans and scratching sounds draw no interest from the night creatures that have observed the precipitous action.

\* \* \* \* \* \*

Hours later, Danny, dark-haired, young, slender visage, troops into a homesteader's poorly tended yard. His response to the suspicious glances of the grizzled old man is to call out, "Like ta buy some grub, mister."

A dog, on the verge of breaking his bonds and hungry enough not to care what type of meal this stranger will make, growls and licks parched lips. The frayed rope barely holding the cur gives little promise of a friendly welcome.

"Got no vittles ta spare, so ya best move on a'for I feed yer stringy meat ta the pigs an' use yer bones fer fertilizer."

"Looks ta me, old man, if you were as good at working the ground as you are at movin' your jaw, you might produce something better than the rock crop you're growing."

"Don't you sass me, boy, or I'll give ya what fer."

From the sorry excuse for a barn, a child struggles under a load that a grown man should be carrying. The old man reaches in the dust beside him for his latigo mule whip.

"I sent you fer them spuds a hour ago, you ungrateful whelp. Guess you need remindin' ta show respect for all my care and goodness."

He coils the whip, preparing his disciplinary tool. The child drops the bundle and cowers at the man's feet. A ribbon of clear skin running from each eye reveals that this is not the first time tears have been shed by the cringing, ragged urchin. Danny pulls from his belt a vintage Navy Colt, browned with rust, but serviceable enough in the focused fifteen-year-old's steady hand as he levels it on the old man's middle.

"No need for corporal punishment when love and Christian compassion is so much more effective." With his back straight, his unwavering grey eyes have the steady look of a man.

The old man stops the back swing of his whip arm. "Easy ta say with that hog leg doin yer negotiatin for ya."

"I often find it useful, settling misunderstandings between the discourse of men."

147

The child scampers to regain equilibrium. "Y'all don't know what you done, mister. He'll flay my hide, soon's yor gone."

The nearly colorless and completely soulless eyes of the old man narrow. "You damn right about that."

Far off in the sage and weed field, vultures fuss and fume, noisily arguing over the best parts of a bloated mule carcass. The youngster looks from one combatant to the other and deep in concentration, forms a hard decision. With a meaningful gesture, shaking the dust from both hands and squinting through overlong bangs at the old man finally comes a response.

"No! I've taken my last beating from you."

The grizzled dirt farmer defiantly casts a gap-toothed grin and responds. "Suit yourself, you hateful pup. But you come with nothin' and, by God you'll leave with nothin'."

Not to be drawn into the dispute, the boy backs carefully toward the foothills from whence he'd come. It's light enough in the open, but once in the aspen groves covering the lush lowlands, it's early twilight and his growling stomach reminds him that he's not solved his most immediate problem. Continuing in a distracted frame of mind is not wise. Downed scrub-oak limbs, exposed twisted roots of Russian Olive and half-hidden rocks are ever-ready villains, waiting to snare an incautious step or thoughtless inattention to surroundings by some pilgrim. It's really too early to bed down, but the few wild onions he'd found are gone and the resident owl's vocal display is sure to keep squirrels from wandering into any trap he might have set. With his canteen dry he's busy gathering moss and leaves for a bed. In the deepening gloom, he's not so absorbed that he doesn't notice the immediate change in air pressure. Something, too silent for a bear, and without the

148

surrounding presence of a wolf pack, has just come into his space.

*Smells like coyote, and without fire, I'm vulnerable.*

His thumb on the hammer, he slips the Colt from his belt, and crouches, waiting. He's prepared for whatever danger might present itself. The actual threat that appears from the shadow is a four-foot-tall biped in ragged scraps and as dirty as a hard-rock miner.

"You followin' me, kid?"

"Nope. Jest mosin' along in the same direction you seem ta be takin'."

He eases the single-action back into his belt and tries to concentrate on his nocturnal preparations, willfully ignoring the child.

"If you fix a fire, I'll share my fish with ya?"

"What? I didn't see any fish in those shallow creeks we passed."

"Don't need ta see 'em, I can sense 'em."

The promise of any food is good; fresh fish is an answer to prayer and makes this communion more interesting. With pine needle kindling and hickory scraps, he quickly has a small but wind-protected fire. By the time it's ready, the largest perch he's ever seen is cleaned and set onto the hot coals. The meal is devoured in silence, as both participants seem not to know what to ask about the other, nor how to phrase questions. Neither is perhaps familiar with human companionship, much less articulate conversation.

* * * * * *

Morning, and the fish bones have been dragged away and polished clean by small scavengers. Danny looks across the clearing to the child's empty pallet. The fire's been stoked into life and the smell of sassafras bark-flavored water from a shallow depression in a flat rock drifts toward him.    He stretches, then moving to the fire, dips a snatchful of long grass into the hot liquid, soaks and then sucks tea from the dripping mass.    From the dark tangles of manzanita, the child appears carrying a double handful of something.    Placing more hot rocks from the fire into the water, the youngster carefully adds the dozen quail eggs into the water.    It brings a grinning response from Danny.    "Having you along is like eating at some fancy Denver buffet table."

When the eggs are done, he uses a forked limb to lifts them out.    The two campers enjoy a meager, but welcome breakfast.

"That old man likely to come for you?"

"Nah, he don't care 'bout me."

"Where're your folks?"

"Ma died 'fore I could remember her."

"How old are you"

"Nine year that I can figger.    But here's brob'ly a couple more 'for that."

"How'd you come to be here?"

"While back, Pa died in a wildfire tryin' ta save our little patch o' grain out Wyomin' way.    We didn't have no water and he tried to beat it out with a blanket. Wasn't enough left ta bury.    Even his bones was so brittle they just powder that the wind blowed away."    He'd sent me into the already burned hills or it woulda got me too. Iffen yo'r headin' south, maybe you won't mind me taggin' along?"

"Well, I'm meeting my father at Butte."

"But that's north, not thisaway."

"I have to take care of a chore first."

"Those tracks yer follow'n?"

"Yeah."

"Two horses and riders, one extra horse?"

"Right."

150

"They're a day ahead. We best be movin' if you 'spect ta catchem 'for the snows come."

Kicking out the fire, they resume their journey and making good time traveling through the day, finally, losing light, they stop for the night and make a quick camp. Along the way, the child has provided for their evening repast. A large Blue Grouse stuffed with wild onions and sage–spitted with a three-foot cedar spike–is set over a low fire.

"I suppose you can sense birds too? Or is it that you outthink them?"

"Fish and birds don't think. They go by natural instinct. So mor'n sense 'em, I figger, if I was a fish, or bird, where would I be? I go and they's there."

Before first light, they're on the trail. The tracks show new, fresh sign and the boy looks forward as often as his head is down, following the hoof prints. During the day they take no rest and work on the supply of pine nuts and wild berries the child hastily gathers along the way.

*  *  *  *  *  *

Late the next day, they're close, but for some reason the boy doesn't want to pursue in full daylight. At a deep, waterfall-blessed creek he strips off his clothes and dives in. The child watches with admiration his graceful strokes and playful enjoyment in the foreign environment.

"Best pile in, wash off that mud. Probably move faster, once you're not carrying twelve pounds of dirt."

"That's okay, I'll scrub down at the shallow part."

"You don't like the deep?"

"I ain't never seen so much water."

He starts to respond, then thinks. "You can't swim."

151

"Never had enough water ta waste, an' that old Granpa never teached me."

The pre-adolescent stares as Danny–naked as the day he entered this world--climbs out onto a large rock and shakes his thin, but muscular body of the excess water.

A casual, light-hearted tone, reveals, "Most ways we's alike. But you got some different parts than me, so I guess iffen you're a boy, I mus' be a girl."

"What?"

"Never seen the difference before."

He sits with legs curled beneath him, contemplating this new information. The fluffy semi-sphere of a cottonwood tree spreading behind him is like a halo.

"Would you like to learn? To swim, I mean?"

The time goes quickly as he gives her a crash course. His teaching method is gentle, but his expectation high. It seems to work, as by the end of the first lesson, she kicks and makes grasping pulls at the surface, but her intrinsic fear of deep water seems to be gone.

After a meal of mushroom and wild parsley-stuffed, clay-wrapped rock chuck eaten in silence, the pair, unfamiliar with small talk, the first feeling of discomfort sets in. Finally, the girl pulls back her hair, revealing an innocent, emotionally unscarred face. "If you'da shot that doe earlier, we wouldn't have ta be eat'in no rodent."

He shrugs. "Only have two rounds and I can't waste them on game."

He watches, wondering if the child will panic at the sight of an approaching six-foot gopher snake. She turns, sees it and throws the greasy remains of the chuck far into the bushes, then stirs the fire to discourage the snake from seeking sleeping accommodations to go with its free meal.

* * * * * *

A chilly, pre-dawn start puts them working toward a campsite showing signs of extreme violence. Creeping forward carefully, they see the reason for the disruption; the eviscerated remains of a horse and only steps away, the badly defiled body of a man.

The boy puts his gun away and the girl looks down at the hollow shell of the corpse. "Cougar would'a dragged the body away ta eat at leisure. He one o' the guys you was achasin?"

"Yeah."

"Most likely a grizzly. Internals was eaten first, then his leg. Coyotes got his face. They go for the eyes and nose first. Kind of a delicacy, I guess."

The boy unbuckles the man's gun belt and Colt .45. He notes the tie-down thong still in place, checks the cartridge-filled cylinder, then slings the rig over his own shoulder. "He never had time to pull his piece."

The girl bends close over the body. "Crows picked at the rest. Under the trees buzzards might not seen him yet. What you think, yesterday?"

"Not much longer."

"No birds in the air, grizzly might still be around, though. We better be movin'."

Danny uses the man's own knife and with a slight hacking motion, removes the man's right index finger and wrapped in a piece of the man's torn shirttail, he stuffs it into his own pocket.

"You collect them things?"

"Nope. This is my first. And he has no more use for it."

Uneasily, the girl looks around. "Shouldn't there be another man and two more horses?"

153

"I wondered about that too, but there's only indication of the one attack. I think his partner was off scrounging firewood when he heard the noise. Bears are not silent killers."

"He just took off, didn't even try to save his friend?"

"They weren't good Samaritan types."

"Does he know you're huntin' him?"

"I doubt it. They left me five days ago with only one swallow of water. He'd expect me to be carrion bait by now."

"Well, he's sure ta be more cautious now."

The boy makes an altruistic offer. "If you'd feel safer going your own way, I'll understand."

"No, I'm good. Besides, I 'spect I'll need another lesson 'fore I kin swim the Snake easy, like you."

He takes a closer look at the small, trusting creature at his side. "My name's Danny, what's yours?"

"Aby. I think it's Abigail. Guess iffen I was smarter, I'da guessed that's a girls name, but I never met no other girls."

"<u>Any</u> other girls. No isn't the right word, Aby."

"All right, Danny." Her wide-eyed look and easy response may unconsciously be the burgeoning feelings of a young girl--fast becoming a woman. "But shouldn't we be on our...Hey, there's blood over here too."

Danny rushes to inspect the scene. "This blood is from his horse."

"How can you tell, Danny?"

"Foam in the blood means a lung puncture." Studying the bent and broken pine branches around the trampled circle, he finds a bloody stub. "He heard or saw the attack and panicked; pulled his horse in a tight turn and ran him into this branch.

That means he's either afoot or he's riding <u>my</u> horse. He won't get far. He's headed up hill and it'll slow him down. If not for that he might have gotten away."

"Won't climbin' slow us down too?"

"Not as much. He's old, must be at least thirty. And he knows how valuable that stallion thoroughbred is. I brought out from Kentucky to improve our herd. It's why they stole him from me. He won't be pushing him hard."

"He might, if he knows you're after him."

"But he doesn't. They left me with only my six-gun and two cartridges. They laughed, said a thirty-six caliber was only good for committing suicide. They left me two bullets, said even holding it up tight against my head, it'd still take two slugs to finish the job."

"I bet you'll only need one o' them when we catch this other hoss thief, Danny."

Then seeing something more in the soft, loamy soil, Danny shows deep concern. "Widespread quadripads moving in the same direction. This is a small, cautious cougar and she might have cubs to worry about."

"If she don't, she'll trail the smell of blood on the air 'till she finds the right place to kill."

They start uphill, following the irregular hoof prints in the soft verdant soil. Less than a half-mile further they crest the ridge, where dim light reveals a sharp cliff falling away to a rock-strewn base a thousand feet below. The twisted, remains of the man's saddled horse lies in a crumpled pile.

"We don't dare get ahead of her or she'll be tracking us."

The girl looks up. "But we can follow close behind. She'll go for the man first. He's a bigger danger."

"I can't gamble on that. I paid more for that stud than our whole ranch is worth."

She slows her breathing and tries to stay calm. "But, Danny, the best mount in the world's not worth your life."

* * * * * *

With cold thin air rasping in their throats and burning their lungs, they follow at a speed more dangerous than prudent. As darkness retreats from the full moon breaking over a far eastern peak, they look down into an arroyo and see the man prostrate, drinking at a shallow creek, slaking a thirst too long neglected. Yards down stream the pewter-grey stallion quivers with excitement. If he realizes his uneasiness is from the undiagnosed smell of mountain cat, he'll panic and on this rocky slope, with eyes bulging, he'll kill himself trying to escape a natural enemy.

Unwilling to disclose their presence with even a whisper, Danny points to the carpet of Kinnikinick ground cover. Aby nods her understanding and avoids stepping on the brittle twigs splayed across the ground like spider webs.

As they watch the horse's sleek coat quiver, an almost undetectable movement and patch of yellow appears on a ledge above the man. Danny pulls his revolver and takes aim. He has a perfect shot; he can kill the man easily. But if he does, the cat will opt for the horse. He adjusts his angle and squeezes the trigger. The girl, with fingers in her ears and eyes closed, hears two shots as one. Wasting no time to see if his quickly aimed deflection shots under unfavorable lighting conditions have hit their marks, he rushes down the slope to grasp the reins of the horse and calm the fidgety stallion. Aby casually climbs down to examine the dead painter, all four legs straddling the boulder. With a quick appraisal, she angles to where the man lays, face submerged in the water. Blood has already stopped oozing from the hole in the back of his head.

She grins at the boy. "Got both with one shot apiece. Guess that thirty-six is good enough after all. You had the forty-five and didn't need it."

"Never even thought of that. I forgot I even had it."

He uses the same knife to remove the second man's trigger finger for his now complete collection. "We best be moseying along. I expect my father will have some ideas about getting you established into the family and planning the proper education for a young lady horse rancher."

Head down, the girl takes a deep breath and softly, as if fearing the answer, "Do you think he'll like me, Danny?"

"Don't see much not to love, Aby."

#

The worldwide danger to our planet is marathon racers. If this threat grows and everybody starts running at the same time and goes West to East they will stop global rotation. Then gravity will no longer work and centrifugal force will throw us all off into space.

#

# 31-THE NIGHT WAS

The night was warm, but the wind found it's way through the narrow crack and a chill breeze washed over her face. She'd cried until there were no tears left. She was wearing her best dress and shoes; it meant nothing to her. Even surrounded by the finest silks and satins that money could buy did nothing to lift her spirits. It would do no good to scream. They would do nothing even if they heard her. It was probably a beautiful night with a bright, full moon and a sky full of sparkling stars; it mattered little, she couldn't see them. She felt herself sinking deeper and deeper. Then a jarring thud and she heard the first shovel-full of dirt hit the lid only inches from her face. But they'd nailed it tight. Nothing could get in...or out.

#
Old men plan wars; young men fight them.
#

# 32-WITCHES <u>CAN</u> COME TRUE

In the living quarters above her shop, Elsbeth carefully lifts an antique volume onto the top shelf of a crowded bookcase. From its old leather and gilt-edged pages, one might assume it's a passed-down family bible. The reverence she shows in her careful handling of the tome seems appropriate for such an heirloom. Sounds of laughter and mirth precede the young couple entering the parlor from the narrow interior stairway. She smiles at her sixteen year-old daughter, Tabatha. Her joy does not extend to her child's greasy-haired companion.

158

"Mrs. M, we been planning this over a week and it's time we came right out and told you how things is."

"Oh, and how is things, Rodger?"

"Well, me and your daughter are gonna' get married. I got a job lined up with a drillin' outfit down in Texas. I figure if I don't getter knocked up first, we'll get hitched someplace along the way. Save money and time thataway. We can live pretty cheap down there."

"I see. And what have you to say about this, Tabatha?"

"Now I know you're probably upset, mama, but we kind of like love each other and need to make our lives together."

"And what about your education? I've arranged your scholarship at Harvard. Will you just throw that away?"

"I thought maybe they'd hold it for me. Else I could transfer it to Lonesome Prairie College. They have online courses at Brownsville I can take."

"I see. And what about you, Rodger? Have you no plans to matriculate in anything but beer guzzling and line dancing?"

"I don't know what the hell that means, but yeah, little edjacation don't do nobody no harm."

"Then there is little else for me to do, but to give you both my blessings. Tabatha, if you'll help me bring in wood for the fireplace, Rodger can go home and get his 1966 Gremlin. That's if he can get it started."

"Sure, mama. I'll pack my things first and be ready to leave as soon as he returns."

The boy leaves with an obscene smirk. Tabatha is still packing when the level of the screeching sound of near-by sirens might easily awaken the dead. The girl goes to the window and sees what has happened.

159

Police cars and ambulances nearly block the view of a rusted and paint starved '66 Gremlin that has apparently tried unsuccessfully to climb a one hundred year old oak tree. Elsbeth is removing clothes from the suitcase and rehanging them in the girl's closet. As recognition seeps into Tabatha's brain, she faints.

\* \* \* \* \* \*

The anticipated Spring tourist crush brings a much-needed influx to the local economy of this tiny coastal town. Elsbeth has hurried to put her antique shop into customer-friendly shape, after the long, dull, New England winter. In the thin sunlight and light offshore breeze, her "Owl and Candle" wooden sign swings with a squeak like a tiny mouse caught in a trap. With a shop full of anxious buyers snatching up items from an historic American period, Elsbeth sips herbal tea and relaxes in a cane rocker while Tabatha rings up sale after sale. Mother and daughter are charmingly dressed in authentic looking seventeenth-century frocks, aprons and caps.

A thin man of indeterminate age and scowling nature enters and brings, somehow, a cloud with him. He shuffles to the counter and berates the mother while simultaneously casting a foul look at the daughter.

"I've told you people before, if you don't keep that dog of yours from howling every night, I'll set the law on you."

"And as I've explained many times, Mr. Windmore, we have no dog. I keep only the one song bird as companion."

"Song bird, SONG BIRD? It's a blasted crow. And it's a nuisance durin' daytime as well. He imitates people talkin'."

He stamps out. Gaslights, horse-drawn carriages and costumed chestnut roasting street vendors, give this charming village a definite Dickensian feel. Unfortunately, some accidents are impossible to avoid. As poor Mr. Windmore crosses the street a runaway horse and buggy strike him down. He dies, mere inches from his front door. Within seconds, this quaint community returns to such calmness; it's as if strife has been outlawed by public proclamation. On the wall shelf behind the vintage cast iron cash register, the pillar and scroll clock strikes one. The next entrant is also, not a customer. Bud Hare is, by his identifying cap, a power company bill collector.

"Mrs. Montgomery, ma'am. We've sent numerous letters explaining that you're overdue with your power usage. Over a month ago we sent another representative to talk to you about it."

"Yes, and he was a most discourteous young man. He became abusive when I explained that there had to be a mistake. I could not possibly have used that much electricity. He wouldn't listen to reason and became most obnoxious. I hope, in the future, your company hires employees with better people skills."

"Well, see, I'm taking his place. He never came back to work. His log states that you were his last contact. After that, he just seems to have disappeared."

"He did impress me as the flighty sort. I expect he moved on to a place more suiting to his ways."

"That may be, but I must take your check back to the office or I'll be fired."

"Can I make you see that I didn't use the amount of electricity you're charging me for?"

"'Fraid not. Our company never makes mistakes."

She takes down a large, dusty, old-fashioned checkbook and with a calligrapher's scroll; she makes out and signs a check for the amount billed. Accepting a receipt, she smiles at the young man.

He takes her check grudgingly, and with all need for courtesy gone, he throws out, "Next time, old lady, pay your bills on time so I won't have to come out to this backwater town again."

He stamps out, slamming the door behind him.

Elsbeth continues dusting and straightening objects, mumbling, "Poor hiring policy is at least <u>one</u> mistake your company makes."

The next day, a giant of a man, near as wide as he is tall enters the "Owl and Candle" and carefully threads his way around furniture, spinning wheels, butter churns, hand made straw brooms, silver urns and a barrel full of gold headed canes. He presents Elsbeth with his business card, Dorian Goslyn, Accounts-New England Power & Light Co. Inc.

"Mrs. Montgomery, I wonder if we might settle this little matter of your electric bill?"

"Oh, but, I paid your Mr. Hare. I don't understand why it hasn't been credited to my account."

He opens and shows her the morning's one-page local paper. It headlines the shocking 1:15 P.M. death of Mr. B. Hare, yesterday, struck by lightning on his way home.

"The shocking part is, you see dear lady, that the sky was clear, with not a single cloud in sight."

"Were you unable to recover my payment from his effects?"

"I'm afraid his clothing and any papers he might have been carrying were burned to a crisp with him."

"But I have a receipt. I always get one when I pay in cash."

"Well, my dear that should put an end to the matter. I'm so sorry to have troubled you."

Only days later, an extremely agitated, pinched-face woman, from customer relations for the power company berates Elsbeth.

"Legal action will be forced if your account isn't immediately brought current."

Slamming her briefcase onto the counter, her face reddened by her agitation, she stands quivering before Elsbeth. Her tirade is answered calmly with a smile.

"But why do you come to me with anger in your eyes and venom on your tongue? I paid your Mr. Hare upon his visit, just the other day. Then your Mr. Goslyn assured me that the matter had been closed. Why do you not speak with him?"

"Can't do that. He moved yesterday to Quebec as general manager of the East Canadian Power Consortium."

"Oh, that's good to hear. He seemed such a nice man."

"Yeah, well I have to take up the slack and this business about you having paid is just plain bunk. It's on a par with 'the dog ate my homework.'"

Elsbeth smiles and excuses herself to wait on a young woman in green scrubs, eying covetously the brass kettle displayed in the window. They are less than twenty feet away when the power company woman clutches her chest and drops like a sack of potatoes thrown from the top of a loaded wagon. The young woman rushes to her side, but finds no pulse.

"I'm a trauma nurse and I'm afraid this woman is dead. Was she a good friend?"

"We were just in the process of becoming close."

"What's her name?"

"I'm afraid we never got that far. We'd only just finished sharing ideas on the importance of presenting a positive business image."

As soon as E.M.T.'s cart the body out to the Black Maria, Elsbeth pulls back an expensive Persian rug and removes the exposed loose floorboards. Holding high a beautifully crafted sterling silver candelabrum, she carefully descends steep and narrow steps. Dim light from the guttering candles is enough to illuminate the dirt-floored basement. She opens the rusty access door of a huge electric furnace, seemingly much larger than needed to heat this average-sized store. From the ashes she removes a die-cast model of a '66 Gremlin and the curled and blackened beanie-baby sized image of a man with a terrified look, two non-descript G.I. Joe-sized dolls with power company caps and a Barbie doll with a tiny, scorched leather briefcase. All are fodder for the trashcan, burned far beyond recognition by anyone less attuned with the circumstance.

Beside the furnace, its power cord is coiled on the ground. The plug is corroded and smashed and is the wrong type for the receptacle on the adjacent wall. Obviously the furnace hasn't been used in decades.


#
There is no proof that Benjamin Franklin ever used an alias when registering with "EHarmony.com."
#

# 33-HE STOLE MY CHICKEN

"That's what I said, twice now, are you hearing impaired?   He stole my chicken and I want you to kill him and get it back for me."

She stood before me, her eyes shooting fire like a Fourth of July pyrotechnic display.

"I don't understand.   I'm a gambler, not the police or even a private detective.   Why come to me?"

"Oh, I know who you are, Mr. Moretti.   I've heard that you get things done; sometimes shady things, illegal things."

"Even if that's true, why should I extend myself on the behalf of a perfect stranger?

"I think I can supply reason enough."

When I didn't respond, she stamped her foot to get my attention.   It set up a rippling effect that did amazing things to a body that would score 15 on anyone's scale of ten. It got my attention.   I took a closer inventory of the diminutive brunette in a crochet dress of a dark blue, almost purple that matched her eyes.   She shook in fury, ready to attack me for even daring to consider refusing her.

I had been, now I was reconsidering.   I pointed to the black leather couch against the wall.

"Please have a seat and tell me more about this "fowl" loss you've suffered."   Blinking as if I'd said something not nearly as funny as I obviously thought, she turned and hip swayed her way across the deep pile carpeting, coiled into a pose to gratify the Playboy photogs.

Crossing one perfect leg over the other in the same motion, she breathed deeply, knowing the strain it put on the dress she'd been poured into. The five-inch heels must have put her on eye level with Mickey Rooney (Michael J. Fox for you nostalgia deficient readers).

"I traced him here to Vegas at four this morning, then lost him at the McCarran Avis counter. I know he's still in town, but he has friends here and I can't handle them all alone. He'll have changed his name, but he rented the car as Jack Williams. Here's his picture and the license plate number." She handed me a list of Vegas addresses. "He's sure to be at one of these places. Get my chicken back first, then we can take him into the desert and waste him. I'll give you a nice reward."

"How much? Since you're proposing this on a strictly business basis."

"It should only take the rest of the morning. It's worth five thousand dollars to me."

"You followed him here from where?"

"That's not important."

As she talked I sought information from the Internet. She hadn't blinked through this discourse and now thought I was completely under her spell and would do whatever she asked. She wasn't far wrong. The computer answer confirmed what I had surmised. I printed out a quick statement and handed it to her to read and sign.

Her eyes threw out sparks that almost ignited my shirtfront. "You must be crazy. You want twenty-five percent of the value when you recover the lost item?"

"Sign it and let's go get the bird. Gee I feel just like Sam Spade looking for the Maltese Falcon."

She stared up at me as if I was a farmer in the middle of the field holding a rope who couldn't decide whether he'd lost a horse or found a rope.   I lifted her by the elbow and guided her to the door.

Stiffening her back she pulled to a stop, threw her head back and with a wave of thick walnut, no, more like chocolate colored hair, demanded,   "You   know?"

"Yes.   Your chicken is about fifteen inches by fifteen inches by fifteen inches; it was cast in 18 karat gold in the late fifties.   You stole it from Peter Dempsey's Golden Rooster Room in Sparks last night. It's only insured for a hundred forty thousand, but the embarrassment value should make it worth half a million. At least that's surely what you're hoping.   Let's go, if you want your chicken back."

* * * * * *

We entered the foyer of an upscale condo building

She hurried ahead to face me.   "Did you bring a gun?"

"No, I depend on brains to accomplish my will. That's why I called ahead."

She looked at me as if viewing a Christian being led happily through the catacombs to visit the lions.

Slipping a graceful hand through my arm, she said, "Yeah, right.   Here, take mine."   She handed me a snub nosed .38 and pushed the penthouse button on the self-service elevator.   "If he gives you any grief, plug him. We can dump the gun.   It's Okay., I have others."

In the executive office, Morrie sat behind a huge teak desk with only spreadsheets, a single cut glass decanter of scotch and matching goblet.   As I asked the all-important question, she snapped handcuffs on his wrists and fastened them to his chair.   He started to answer, but she pulled an air horn from her purse, shoved it in his ear and let blast.   He crumpled like a Macy's balloon after the Thanksgiving Day Parade.

"What are you doing?   He was ready to tell us what he knew."

"It would have been a lie.   Even a dyslexic Boy Scout could tell that."

He opened his mouth and she hit the air horn again. "Try it now, he might be more conducive to telling the truth this time."   He just sat there in a daze.   His ears must have been ringing so loud he'd hear nothing for days.   She wasn't very patient.   "Let's off him and go on to the next one on our list."

"No.   We'll hear what he has to say, then I'll decide if we go on."

"Okay, but don't waste time, we're burning daylight."

He was still slow in answering.   She found a silver cigarette lighter, poured his Scotch onto the desk and put flame to it.   It was ablaze before I could react, and cuffed to the chair he was unable to get away.   In a second, the smell of his burning eyebrows and toupee filled the room.

On our way out, Stumpy, the bodyguard with the brains of a cucumber, still figured he shouldn't let us go. She seemed to faint and Stumpy caught her.   Putting her entire ninety-eight pounds into it, she drove a stiletto heel into his left instep.   The sound of bones crunching echoed off the harsh walls of the anteroom.   Our further progress was thus unencumbered.   Well, that's it."

"What do you mean that's it?   What happened next?"

"Oh, we tried a few more places, but with too much time and distance between the chicken and us, it was a waste of time.   I've since heard the Nugget got it back."

"And the girl?   What about her?"

"Never saw her again.   Pity, too.   She was some kind of looker."

## PART II

Jim Ficker, the reporter for "Las Vegas Life" didn't look convinced.   Just then she entered, carried champagne in a silver ice bucket and a platter of crab puffs.   She wore a zebra-striped jump suit that made my eyeballs jump.   She came over and kissed me, then shoved a crab puff in my mouth and turned to Jim.

"So, you're going to print the story he gave you? Well, I guess it's not my job to keep the press accurate." She started back toward the kitchen.

"Miss. Ms,…or does something else now preface Laurel Jamison?"

"That's not important.   You want the story behind the chicken, right?   Well, he probably slanted the truth to make it come out the way he wants.   I'll put it into proper perspective if you like."

I sighed, knowing no straight man between six and a hundred and six would refuse an opportunity to spend time with her.   I also knew that she loved having an audience of worshipful admirers.   I poured myself champagne and went into my study.   I shut the door, not wanting to be an impediment to her version of the truth. With Beethoven's Eroica at high volume I'd not be tempted to eaves drop.

\* \* \* \* \* \*

I opened my notepad and held my pen at the ready. She gave me champagne, a crab puff and poured herself into a demure pose on the couch opposite, giving me thoughts of latent sexuality and a glimpse of school girl innocence.   She could do the one with her body and the other with eyes that could go from Elvira to Dorothy in Oz faster than a hummingbird's heartbeat.

"It started when I was led unknowingly into a cabal plan to steal the chicken. I had to draw the crowd's attention. Naturally I didn't know the reason at the time. When I learned what they'd done, I had to get it back and return it to protect my reputation and stay out of jail. I'd heard about Ken's ability to get things done and asked for his help. He agreed and used non-confrontational methods to recover the bird. When it was returned, Peter Dempsey agreed not to press charges and even gave us a fifty thousand dollar reward. I'm just glad it turned out all right and my reputation is still clean."

"Then the rumor that you master minded the operation and when they skipped out with the prize you swore to get it back and wreak havoc on the traitors is false?"

With that she went into her Dorothy-not in Kansas-anymore mode. "Do I look like a vengeful creature to you?"

What could I do?

"Then why are you still here? They paid you a reward?"

"Well, I'd agreed to give Ken 25%. He said I could keep it all and become his assistant. I had nowhere better to go, so…"

"So to quote Ira Gershwin…It's Summer time and the livin' is easy."

Brushing back a wing of roasted chestnut colored mane from one eye, she uncoiled herself from the couch and came to offer her hand. With a sigh and the last draught of champagne, I stood and regrettably took my leave.

170

## PART III

I left the rambling twenty-room estate overlooking the Vegas strip below and drove my '93 Honda, slowly past the four-car garage. Only the V12 Jag and two Lamborghini convertibles were in view. All the way down to the desert floor I considered what I could and would write. At the walkup offices of "Las Vegas Life," the entertainment rag that calls itself a journalistic endeavor, I still hadn't decided. In my seven by nine office I turned on the swamp cooler, pulled off my jacket and flicked on a four-year-old computer.

After three hours, I carried a single page to my boss.

"What the hell is this? You've been on this three weeks, way over budget, and you say, "Rumors of the theft of the Golden Rooster are in error. With the Golden Rooster Room shut down for remodeling, the art object had been removed for safekeeping."

I smiled. "If I print the truth, Ken will own this magazine. There were three involved; a janitor, a guy in security and Laurel. She'd planned the whole thing. She would cause a distraction. They needed twenty seconds. She played craps, in a very low cut gown. Some guy supposedly bumped her and her top came down. Naturally, she straightened up topless. That was good for twenty seconds alone. But she ooed and ahhed while fumbling her self back under cover. Something she surely could have done with much more finesse than she showed. Another ten seconds. Then she yelled that someone had cut the straps of her dress, the one she was trying very inefficiently to hold together. Another ten seconds. Then she screamed that he'd also stolen her purse. Security stopped everybody carrying a black

171

purse. 'Course the guys were all still watching her; which was just as good.

With everybody focused either on her or the exits, the janitor grabbed the chicken."

"How did they get it away? There must have been an alarm system."

"Yeah, and it worked. But the Casino recycles all cardboard. They'd previously cut the center out of a stack. The janitor shoved the rooster into the middle, banded and marked the stack, then put it out on the dock with the others. After the furor calmed, they just came back with a truck and got the marked stack."

"So how did it get to Vegas?"

"The janitor quit and hopped a plane with it, sold it to a fence here in Vegas. Not in her plans at all. The security guard hasn't been heard from since and the janitor's gone missing as well. This is not the kind of gal you want to cross."

"So you think she bumped them both off? Or was it this Ken?"

"Don't know, but she could tell the story fifty ways and you'd believe each version."

"She's that good?"

"She could teach an Indian fakir how to charm snakes without a flute."

"So if they returned the rooster, nobody would take exception to the story."

"Not if that's the end of the story. But between the time he recovered the bird and returned it to the Nugget he made a fast trip to Mexico. And before he left, he contacted a gold broker; and a fashion jeweler who casts objects in wax, then has the final pieces cast in gold in Mexico."

172

"So you figure he made a duplicate? That's pure conjecture. And even if he did, it may be tacky, but it's not illegal."

"Not if he returned the original and kept the duplicate. I can't write that story because I can't prove it either way."

"Does she know?

"Wouldn't tell us if she did. She's some piece of work. She was wearing a jump suit so tight if she had hyperventilated she'd have burst the seams. But it covered all the parts you think shouldn't be covered. I mean clinically it was modest enough that I'd have introduced her to my mother. Not my father. He'd have had dreams for months that he wouldn't dare tell the priest about."

#

Coming between a hungry lion and a side of
beef is usually smarter and safer than coming
between a mother and her child.

#

# 34-PEACE ON EARTH, GOOD WILL TOWARD MEN

Reporters crowd the steps of the new White House in "Heart of America," a small Kansas town. The president has just finished his first State of the Union Speech and now, on the veranda, in smoking jacket and soft slippers, sprawled in a rattan chair, enjoying a Scotch and soda, he looks down on an adoring press corps, print and media journalists. Television and radio lines are fed directly to satellites for worldwide distribution. This question and answer portion is designed to clarify any areas of confusion. The representative from American

Press International looks as though he can't believe the question he's just asked.

The President smiles condescendingly. "That's right, John. I meant <u>exactly</u> what I said. We must close ranks to heal the divisions that have held this country apart far too long. A problem never dealt with by the Democrats OR Republicans, but one which my party, the party of the people, the party of the twenty-first century, the Unitarian party, will solve."

"But, Mr. President, giving away land belonging to sovereign states? It's unprecedented. It's...it's..."

"John, didn't the nineties teach us that we MUST be sensitive to the needs of others? We have ignored our better instincts, fed our own greedy desires and self interests long enough. Here and now it ends. As caring, feeling, loving humans, brothers on this old earth, I pledge to do all I can to return this nation to calm thought and rational action."

"By giving..."

"Don't think of it as giving. Think of it as sharing."

"But Georgia, Alabama, Arkansas and Mississippi, the entire south..."

"Ah, there you're wrong, John. The Deep South includes Florida and Louisiana. And anyway you know that eventually Fairy Louicon's continued agitating would bring on another civil war to tear this great nation apart."

"Frank, Universal Television?"

"Yes, Mr. President, it's true that you didn't include those two states in the offer to the Nation of Aslam, but you gave the Cubans Florida and Louisiana to the French Cajuns."

"The Cubans have squatter's rights half way to Jacksonville already and the French have run New Orleans de-facto for centuries and where else could you get better Jambalaya?"

174

"Jeffers from...I.B.S. Network?"

"And what about Oklahoma, Nebraska and the Dakotas, Mr. President? You've ceded those to the Native American tribes."

"Jeffers, Jeffers, have you no social conscience? Can we enjoy so many God-given luxuries while our good neighbors live in squalor? We cheated them out of this entire continent. We ARE our brother's keeper. Andy, pass out those statistical charts showing how this country can become more productive if we don't have to carry so many revenue-draining states."

Jeffers responds with, "Like Hawaii, sir? You propose to give Japan an outright deed to the islands. And what about Michigan? You want to turn that over to Canada."

"Well, the sons of Nippon have bought up most of the Islands already, and do we really need Michigan? As I recall, you drive an Infinity, Sam. My limo is a BMW."

"Ms Macho, Lesbian National Press?"

"Mr. President, my paper backed your candidacy and I personally voted for you, but you've given Alaska back to Russia."

"They asked for it, and let's be honest here. We paid them nothing and drained it of all its natural resources."

"Mr. Chang, New Sino Network. Now don't tell me YOU have a problem with this? After all, your people came over as sing-songing coolies and built the railroads that link the coasts. I gave you Washington and Oregon, some great fishing up there. If you want another option, Bill Gates will probably buy them back."

Jeffers cuts in with, "But that's not all. You're turning over Maine, Vermont and New Hampshire to Canada as well."

175

"Sure, when's the last time you craved a moose burger? And who can't live without maple syrup? Pancakes aren't good for you anyway."

"That doesn't take into account Wisconsin and Minnesota. We have..."

"People, people, work with me here. We can live very well in this new streamlined entity; have a more responsive central government with a shorter, more direct connection to the people."

"Ms Young, San Francisco Enquirer?"

"Yes, Mr. President. You say the Cubans have squatter's rights. Does that also relate to the illegal masses swarming across our southern border? You've given them Texas and New Mexico."

"Well, have you ever been to either of those places in summer?"

"But within the hour, according to my satellite link, President Gonzales claims they must have California as well."

"WHAT? I just bought ten acres in Malibu and those sleazy beaners want to take it from ME? No damn way. General! Scramble those B1B's on stand-by at Nellis and Edwards. Let's Nuke those ungrateful wetbacks."

"Mr. President?"

"And get those armed Wright-Patterson FA18's airborne. Might as well hit Quebec the same time. Those frogs are the only canucks we'd have problems with. We take out the bead-janglers and the rest will collapse. Forty gazillion acres of useless snow will be ours."

"Mr. President, surely we can't start a simultaneous war with Mexico and Canada."

"Why not? The chili-poppers only have Saturday night specials and home made pipe guns. Sure, they may have a few street sweepers, but they can't hit anything unless it's in a drive by and they usually can't get their cars started anyway.  Up north, the Maple-leaf rubes have turned-in all but their squirrel rifles.  We'll make the raid on Libya look like the hundred year war.  By God, I feel young again.  This is just what we need to draw us closer together, a good old fashioned war we can all get behind."

The telephone lines to the TV remote vans catch fire with overload from outgoing signal and incoming calls from world leaders.  Armed Secret Service and worried Cabinet members lead the president inside.  He alone smiles with the serene confidence of those who know they are on a mission of salvation to the less informed, the…unenlightened.

#

Did you ever wonder why there's no Olympic
event for square dancing, yodeling or accordion
playing?  Yeah, me neither.

#

# 35-HOW TO BE HAPPY

The subway was crowded; I was standing, holding the anti-sway strap.  With the hypnotic rumble of the wheels and the rhythmic side-to-side motion of the car there was little to do or think about.  Then I noticed the woman standing next to me.  It's hard not to notice others when you're bodies are apt to touch in several familiar junctures on a regular basis.  Had it not been for the book she was reading my mind might have gone off on another tangent.  But as it was, I fixated on her book and what it meant.  It was titled 'How to be Completely Happy All the Time.'  At that point I realized that I had been given

177

an answer to a dilemma that has puzzled civilization since the beginning of time.

## Women EXPECT to be happy! They consider it their due!

Men are much different in this regard. If, when a man awakes he remembers where he is; crawls out of bed and nothing hurts more than it did when he got into bed; he doesn't scald his tongue on MacDonald's coffee; or choke on an egg shell in his breakfast burrito; his car isn't stolen from the parking lot; he isn't fired for losing a paper clip in the office computer; his cigarette cough doesn't get any worse; his rent check doesn't bounce; his credit card isn't rejected for ordering that hair piece from 'Twenty Again and Loving It'; he doesn't get a card from his doctor showing his PSA; cholesterol and blood pressure are all near the one thousand mark; his mother doesn't want to come for Christmas with her new twenty year old unemployed poet boyfriend; the dog doesn't bite him; he's not allergic to beer; his auto insurance premium isn't being raised because he ran over that Hare-Krishna; the medication he's taking for nerves doesn't cause him to grow breasts; his subscription to Playboy isn't cancelled; the mole on his cheek doesn't turn color or get larger; he can sleep the night with only six or seven trips to the bathroom; he receives a free life time supply of Viagra and just as he trades in his 12 mile a gallon car for one that gets 42; the price goes up another sixty cents a gallon; he's happy.

If I had a nickel for every time I've regretted
not studying harder, eating more vegetables,
exercising, getting more sleep and writing
poetry over the last fifty years I'd have…Oh,
lets see, maybe fifteen cents.

#

# 36-RIGHT TIME, RIGHT PLACE

Johnny sits at the worn, stale beer smelling bar, his feet hooked around the stools' spreader-bar. He raises his empty glass and the bartender brings him Jack Daniel, water back. At the port end of the bar an obnoxious broker drinks Glen Livet neat. Must have been a good day in the market, he's not even trying to hustle any business. At the starboard end, two young men, (too pretty to be straight) sip white wine spritzers and frown. Johnny overhears more of their lover's quarrel than he wants. They're out of place in this blue-collar bar; better had they just kissed and moved on. With no jukebox or open mike, this eastern Idaho establishment is for the rapid and constant consumption of alcohol. So with the sudden and simultaneous intake of breath from all the patrons you'd think Johnny would look around. He doesn't. He doesn't even check the back-bar mirror. He doesn't have to. He can hear the strike of her heels on the asphalt-tiled floor and smell her tuber rose perfume.
She saunters to the bar, is about to order, when a leather-jacketed, greasy-haired tough, from a gaggle of others of similar ilk, slinks to her side.

"Buy you a drink, gorgeous?"

Johnny stands, picks up a stool as if he's moving it along the bar. Using only half his upper body strength, he sets one steel tubular leg down on the instep of the tough.

"The lady's not interested, punk.   So take your posse someplace you can frighten little kids and octogenarians."

No one else in the bar is aware of what is happening.   The youth winces in pain.

"You can't..."

"What, break your foot?   Already done that. You'll only limp for a month or two.   But if I press just a scooch more you'll never walk straight again."

He lifts the stool and lets the youth stagger back to his table where his gang helps him out to the street. Johnny still hasn't even looked at her.   A shame, she'd hold every male's attention even during a Victoria's Secret lingerie modeling.

She whispers, "I guess I owe you a drink even though..."

He holds up his glass.   "Got one, but you can do something, more for yourself than for me."

She looks askance but with her arms resting on the edge of the bar, she's busy settling herself onto a stool when the jaws of a steel claw capture her right wrist.   A faint click is heard, but the sound travels no further then a few feet.   Johnny's left hand ratchets it tight enough to assure compliance, not enough to cut off circulation.

"What are you...?"

"Sh, outside.   Let the crowd see that I must have the most miraculous pick-up line in history."

He throws a ten on the bar and slides off his stool; she has no choice but to follow.   His first appraisal of her face and figure are off the scale and their departure is marked by disbelief from all patrons.   Outside, she baulks, finally, as he puts her into his car and handcuffs her to the door.

"This is where your partner arrives and takes all my valuables. This time there's a change of plan. When he shows up you'll act as if nothing is wrong. Then he'll be arrested and you'll go free. You just have to keep quiet until it's over."

"But, I don't know…"

"What did I just say?"

He shuts the passenger door as a tall, trench-coated man, hands deep in his coat pockets approaches. Before he can say anything, Johnny pulls a gigantic revolver from behind his back.

"Don't even inhale."

He cuffs the man's wrists behind his back and around a lamppost. Returning to his car, an older, non-descript Plymouth sedan, he puts the claw into the glove compartment and removes a small handgun.

The man, with a bemused grin says, "You got nothing on me, I'm never armed, it's just a bluff."

Wiping the gun of fingerprints, he unloads it and wraps the man's right hand around it.

"I'm calling that bluff. Now, if you take your punishment like a good little boy and don't involve the woman, I won't be forced to say I took this gun from you. It means the difference between a two or ten years sentence."

A large plainclothes officer, gold badge affixed to his breast pocket, arrives and sees the situation. He responds with a frown.

"You were supposed to wait for me, not make any overt move, Johnny."

"He was too quick off the blocks, but you had things wrong, Captain. The girl was no part of it. She's an innocent victim as well."

"The hell you mean? She's his niece. They've been working together over a year, used the stolen credit cards to finance their lifestyle. She's got a record of five arrests."

"Petty larceny, when she was young. Four dismissed and one probation, which she served. This time she was being held against her will. She shouldn't even be forced to testify. He got all the money. She told me the whole thing."

"How'd you get her to do that? You use that claw on her?"

"Captain, you know that's illegal, and I'm not on the force anymore, just a simple civilian you asked to watch out for them. Glad I could do my part."

"Okay, we've got <u>him</u> dead bang. None of the vics put her as part of the scam. They all say it looked like she was being robbed as well. But we both know better."

The Captain takes the man into custody and as he's leading his prisoner away, looks back to Johnny. "What are you going to do with her?"

"Oh, I'll drive her home; see her safely tucked in."

When he starts the Plymouth the woman is still glaring at him. Her long dark hair dances happily about her shoulders, but there's fire in her eyes.

"Why are you doing this? You don't even know me."

"Sure I do. I've read your file. This time you'd have taken a hard fall and you're too pleasant looking to enjoy prison life. So I'll take you home and you can start a new life."

"I don't have a home. We're staying in a couple of rooms at the Motel 6."

He pulls the car into light traffic.

"I didn't mean <u>your</u> home. I have a spare bedroom and you can take your pick. Can you cook?"

"No, but…"

"That's okay, I'll teach you.   I can boil water. Everything else you can learn from cookbooks.   Martha Stewart gave me a ton of them before she went in."

As the scene of her narrow escape from prison fades behind her, the fire in her eyes, this time is more like sparkle.   She moves over closer to him.

I'd say it pays to be in the right place at the right time.

#
The rumor that Calvin Coolidge was the ghostwriter for three of Jacqueline Sussan's books has yet to be verified.
#

# 37-THE PERSONAL COST OF IGNORING SCIENCE

Albert turned and looked back at the silhouette of the four-master he'd abandoned.   The furled sails in the slack water meant nothing.   He'd left it to prove his theory that science, as we know it, is wrong.   The "red sky in the morning, sailor take warning, red sky at night, sailor's delight" was another adage that had no basis in fact.   Another old wives tale, if you will, is what he was about to decry.   The inaccuracy of one of those unproven tenets, the myth that the world was round.   He rowed ever westward, sinewy arms straining with every stroke that drove the boat forward another seven feet.   Seven feet closer to his being acknowledged by the nautical and cartographer's world as a myth-buster.   He glanced quickly into the blue-black of the uncharted western darkness where sea and sky merge and the unverified existed.

183

In the distant eastern horizon, the pre-dawn rays were just beginning to creep over the black water. His eyes were again drawn to the thin line of life-affirming blue. Then just within seconds below that, bright rose and then spreading below that a new days' harsh, unforgiving, cadmium yellow--the God of light--sprang above the deep black/green of ocean.

Aboard the "Champlain," another check mark is made on the bulkhead calendar in the Captain's cabin. With the Man-o-War at anchor, the entire crew lined the deck rail and looked into the western darkness, straining to see the ever-decreasing tiny spec upon the distant surface.

With little regard for his waning strength, Albert continued straining at the oars, propelling the barely sea-worthy craft toward the unknown. He alone would prove the earth was round. As the star-studded dark western sky shone above, giving the counterfeit illusion of safety, he threw his body forward for another oar's grasp at the sea.

His final thought came to him as he and the boat went over the edge and fell into utter, empty darkness and silence.

*I've been right and the others were wrong.*

Watching from the bridge and benefited by the use of telescopes, the officers saw the craft tip into space. As one they felt that Albert might better off, if not as quickly or as bloodlessly, have been swallowed by a giant sea monster.

# 38-MUCH TO REMEMBER

*The last thing I recall is the car swerving out of control on that icy curved road from Challis. I heard the rear wheels spinning and the transmission revving, next some sort of squeal as the car lost traction. Then we were off the road, over the embankment and falling. The sky was above, then below, overhead again. Then...nothing until just now, with my eyes straining to see form in the dimly lit whiteness and antiseptic-smelling surroundings. Somewhere in the distance there's a sort of annoying muted gong, then the squish of footsteps and a change in air pressure that seems to announce another's presence. Where was I? What had happened? How did I get here?*

The face of an angel in white appears within my vision and smiles down at me.

"Mr. Baxter? How are you feeling? Can I get you anything?"

*The light behind her causes a halo around her. She's an angel to me, but she's obviously also a nurse.*

"You can tell me where I am and what happened?"

"You were in an accident and pretty banged up. This is the Sawtooth Sanitorium."

"What about my wife, Margarette? She was with me in the car. Is she all right?"

185

"Your wife...suffered only bruises and scratches in the accident."

*Then there are others, surrounding me, quietly taking station in a circle.*

My angel turns and motions them all silently out. "I'm going to get the doctor, now you just rest, I'll be right outside."

She disappears, but when I turn my head I can see her at the nurses' station. She's speaking into a small instrument. A doctor, wiping crumbs from his mouth, hurries toward her. He puts down a coffee cup and takes up a medical file, swivels his head to gaze in my direction. After a few minutes he comes to stand over me. Fitting a stethoscope to his ears and pulling tubes from my arm, he listens to my heart and makes notes in a file.

"Doctor, I need to see my wife and..."

"Uh, I believe Nurse Cooper is making arrangements with your family now."

He leaves, but orderlies and other nurses are still looking at me. It seems like a year until Nurse Cooper (my angel) returns.

"Mr. Baxter, there are some anxious people here to see you. They've been very concerned about you."

She dashes away before I can ask her anything else. A very pretty young woman, about thirty or so hands her large dark-blue purse to a tall man standing behind her. She approaches and takes my hand in both hers.

"Do I know you, miss?"

She smiles down at me, but her lips seem to be quivering and she tries several times before she can get words out and when she does they're tremulous.

"Yes, now I know this will sound like a movie, but..." She turns and takes her purse from the man,

186

fumbles inside for a leather wallet. "You were in a car accident. You had a concussion and…"

"I know that, but you said…"

She pulls a photo from the wallet and holds it under my nose. It's a photo of Marg, me and little Julie posed in front of my new Pontiac Chief hard-top.

"Where's Marg? I need to see her, to know that she's all right. I'm confused."

"That photo was taken just before you left for Boise. That was the trip where you slid off the road in November 1977. Its 2007 now, dad. You've been in a coma for thirty years."

*She looks to be normal, why would a hospital allow a crazy woman to just wander around like this?*

My angel/nurse comes to stand beside the crazy woman who is trying hard to hold back tears. "She's right, Mr. Baxter. This is your daughter Julie."

*I look back at the young woman who does seem vaguely to resemble my beloved three year old.*

"I'll come back later and bring the girls. You have three granddaughters, dad. You should rest now."

"If what you say is correct I've had thirty years of rest. Now dammit, where's Marg? Can I see her?"

She pulls another photo and shows me an attractive woman just entering middle age.

"This is mom three years ago, just before she died of cancer."

"This is some trick. You're trying to make me think I'm crazy. You're after my money."

She takes something else from her purse and hands it to me. It's a small mirror. The last mirror I looked into reflected a twenty-eight year old with smooth skin and a head full of dark brown hair. The face looking back at me is wrinkled and has a receding hairline of short grey stubble. I try hard to get a full breath, but I can't argue any more. I hand the mirror back, but don't look up at her. I must have gotten some dust in my eye. Finally I form my response.

"Three granddaughters you say? I hope at least one of them looks like your mother."

#

Contrary to common belief, crocodiles do NOT<br>make good pets in high-rise apartments.

#

# 39-SAFETY INSTRUCTIONS

Just like many of you other frequent fliers, I usually sleep, read or do crossword puzzles while instructions for emergency procedures are given. I stash my carry-on in the overhead compartment and never smoke in the toilets, nor do I use electronic equipment during take-off and landing, I keep my tray up, always fasten my seat-belt and never ask for more than the three ounces of liquid refreshment and the bag with seven peanuts that you can't open anyway and I keep my seat in the upright position. That should qualify me for at least one attaboy, right?

That's what I thought too. Then I boarded Flight 666 leaving Denver for Oakland on a bright, sunny August noon. Everything went by the book and I looked forward to being met at the airport by my wife. We'd have a great seafood dinner at Jack London Square; maybe take in a movie downtown, something we've seldom done lately. I was preparing to reset my watch to accommodate the one-hour difference between Mountain and Pacific Coast time. These were my thoughts at 3:14. Then, at 3:14-1/2 everything changed.

I remember the cabin lights going out as a great flash came from outside, then we were going down at a

188

steep angle. I knew freak thunderstorms can happen over the Rockies this time of the year and I can think about these things rationally now. At the time, I and probably everybody else aboard, knew only panic.

The pilot had last announced our altitude as 3500 feet and I think it took us about fifteen minutes to climb to that station. We came down in what seemed like fifteen seconds. Just enough time to pray, not enough time to regret not telling all the people you care for that you love them.

How it happened, I don't know, but somehow the pilots were able to level out the plane just before touchdown. Our reconnection with the surface was rough and wet, but given the alternative of being compressed into a five-foot aluminum ball, nothing to complain about.

At this point, with everyone feeling, touching or pinching various body parts to assure that life still existed; we began to resume normal brain functions. Then is when I regretted not having paid closer attention to the safety instructions. All the other passengers, it seems had placed masks over their faces and fitted their individual lifejackets in place and as soon as it was clear that we'd made a water landing, they were all inflated. I, on the other hand, being untethered, might have easily made my way to the emergency exit. Except trying to fight my way to the aisle, was like climbing through a dark cave filled with a maze of spider webs. No one else beat me to the exit though. All the others were grabbing their carry on luggage, fighting seatbelts, oxygen lines, and inflated floatation devices within the confined space of economy seating.

Now reading this, you've figured out that I lived through the ordeal. Interestingly, though, the part none of us realized until we assembled on the wings was that we'd landed in the middle of the Great Salt Lake. The plane floated like a raft at summer camp. And because no emergency radio message had been sent when the plane went down, no one knew we were missing. So there we sat for almost forty hours. After the first twenty, I swore I'd handle my own safety. From now on, I'll carry my own one-man life raft and I'll never, never, never eat another peanut or pretzel in my life.

#

How good can a quarterback's fingers taste?
He licks them all throughout the game.

#

# 40-TEQUILLA DREAMS

I <u>had</u> to do it and doing anything I don't like doing <u>cheerfully</u> is not in my nature. I'd been told she'd be there when I arrived and I wouldn't need a description. I'd not be able to miss her. First of all, I hate ambiguity in most forms, more so with my life or safety at risk. I pressed for more intel, but was told I had all I needed and to just carry out my assignment without more questions.

So there I was in Reynosa, Mexico on a sweltering August twilight looking for someone I didn't know and was sure I wouldn't like when finally we met. I'm a hair over six feet, have spent all of my adult life in dangerous situations, but usually with some knowledge of what I was up against before it became too deep for extrication. Well, I may not be happy about it, but God willing, I'd start it and I'd finish it.

From a distance of fifty yards you could see the Red Pepper bar and grille inhaling and exhaling stale, sweaty, beer-smelling cigarette smoke as the crowd ingress and egress fluctuated. It was like a living creature giving off

190

fog-breath in freezing weather.    But it was over a hundred degrees.    Even in my hotel room, the A/C ran 24/7 just to keep it below eighty.    At night I'd turn it off and keep the window wide open.    There was a slight breeze off the water, but the Gulf humidity jumped a percentage point per minute.

I shouldered my way through the entrance and as my eyes grew accustomed to the dim lighting, I eased up to the bar and signaled for Tequila.    I hadn't even finished a cursory look around the room when I saw her. Some of the bar flies were young and not bad looking, but on a scale of ten, they were a 6 on the scale that she'd have broken at twenty.    I carried my drink to her table, took the seat opposite and got a close-up look at the woman.    She probably wouldn't see twenty-five again, but she'd have beaten out all the eighteen-year olds in a Miss Universe Contest.  She was sitting crosswise on her chair; black leather boot encased long legs crossed.    She didn't bother looking up and waved me off with a gesture that carried the idea that I was trash, only fit to be carried out by some lower life.

When I made no sound or gesture to move, her fathomless black eyes finally dained to honor me with a glance, they seemed to grow just a bit larger.    Then they too, in a completely dismissive way, refused to acknowledge my presence, until finally.    "I'm not lonely, so just ride off, cowboy, I'll send your saddle home."

She spoke perfect, accent less English.    She might have had some Caucasian blood somewhere in the dim past, but it only showed in her voice and milk chocolate complexion.    The bar girl arrived silently and set a drink before the woman.

"From the tall one in the corner.    He wishes you to join him and his friends."

191

Before she could voice her response, I turned the glass over, forcing the contents to puddle on the table, then to spill onto the sawdust-covered floor.

I held up my own glass.

"Bring us an unopened bottle."

This time the woman did acknowledge me with a look that held no welcome, but slightly less contempt. The man in the corner saw the poor reception his offering had received. He now advanced, slid into the seat to my left. He wasn't just tall; he was big. Big, ugly and mean looking. Obviously he'd never heard about not bringing a knife to a gunfight. His smile seemed warm and friendly; the six-inch stiletto he held just above the table didn't.

"The Colt I'm aiming at your middle sends lead cross country at twelve hundred feet per second. You're about a foot away. It'll take one twelve-hundredth of a second to reach you. If you think you're fast enough to beat that, go ahead."

"I think, Senor, you are bluffing."

The explosion of the shot echoed through the room several times before the ringing in everyone's ears began to dissipate. His beady eyes swelled to near bursting as he jumped up, knocking his chair backwards. He saw, at the bottom of the chair, a .45 caliber hole half an inch from his privates.

"I should remember to correct my aim. It shoots a half-inch low at this distance. I hope there will be no more interruptions."

The speed with which he backed away, followed by six of his cohorts, was answer enough. The rest of the bar's patrons studiously ignored us. I turned back to appreciate the respectful look she was giving me, I refilled our glasses and moved my chair closer. It gave me a better view of the room and...her.

"What's your business, Mr...?"

"Import and export."

"Really, and what do you export?"

"American dollars."

"And you import...?"

"Your greatest national treasure."

"Pre-Columbian artifacts or more modern goods, like Aztec gold?"

"No, I'm not an art dealer and have no interested in organic stimuli."

"Then why are you here, putting yourself in harm's way? This is not a place for the average tourist."

"I was told that you could get me the goods I seek."

"And that would be?"

"I think you already know. I need twelve girls. Young, pretty, unattached, clean. I'll pay twelve-thousand dollars, plus a brokerage fee of another thousand each."

"You are mistaken. Your informants have misled you. I am not in business of any kind."

"Undoubtedly, but I sense that while you are completely innocent of any knowledge of which I speak, you seem, never the less, resourceful enough to attend to my needs."

"And you want these girls for...what? Immoral purposes?"

"Never. I have wealthy American clients who desire household workers that are easy on the eyes. When they entertain, they don't want some ugly old crone upsetting the delicate constitution of their guests."

"These girls would then be offered work visas or green cards?"

"That's beyond my knowledge, but at some point it would seem possible."

She stared as if trying to see through my eyes into my soul. I was afraid that given time, she might. We drank from the new bottle and silence prevailed for an eternity or two.

As a brawl in the far corner broke the impasse, she sat up straighter and must have come to a decision, because she wrote down a phone number on a napkin and handed it to me. I tore it up, dropped the pieces into my glass and drank it down. I stood and lifted her to her feet.

"There's no need for long distant communications. Until I take possession of the merchandise on the other side of the border, you'll not be leaving my sight."

"You surely don't expect me to…"

"I think it's perfectly obvious that I will deliver the cash to you and you alone. Let us enjoy a promenade along the shore, we shall feel the cool of the evening breeze and the soothing sounds of the lapping waves."

She was loath to come with me, but she came. After an hour's stroll amid jasmine filled air I was in a mood to forgive her almost anything. Okay, anything. She tried to break free twice, but my arm around her waist grew tighter with each attempt. Back in my hotel room, with raw oysters, lobster, champagne and chocolate decadence from room service she seemed slightly more relaxed, but still wary.

"You can call anybody you like as long as you give only specifics on what and when. I'll supply the where at the last minute."

"But, you can't expect me to get twelve girls across the border without drawing attention."

"I've already taken care of that. I'll have Junior Dallas Cowboy Cheerleader uniforms waiting as soon as you tell me you're ready. The girls will not only pass muster, they'll be escorted through with applause and cameras."

194

I listened as she made her calls to be assured she didn't give away our location.

"The door is locked and wedged; we're on the fourth floor and there's no fire escape. You'll be safe if you don't do anything stupid. Naturally I'm not going to give up my bed. There's a pillow and sheets. I hope you'll be comfortable on the sofa. I'll take my shower first, you can use it next."

"Maybe I could borrow a tee shirt?"

"Mine are 40-regular, I'm not sure they'll fit you."

"I'm good at coping with adversity. They'll probably stretch."

That was the last I saw of her that night. The lights were off and the drapes drawn when I finished my shower and slid into bed. I heard her enter the bathroom, and tried to stay awake, but soon drifted off. When she slipped into bed beside me and I felt warm flesh touching every important part of my body, I came wide-awake.

"The T shirt didn't stretch. You never said you wouldn't share the bed, but if I'm crowding you…"

She started to move away. My arm stopped her and brought her back to the skin-on skin contact.

In the morning, she seemed less standoffish than when we first met. Close companionship, sharing furniture and underwear can have that effect on a relationship.

"Okay, my people have delivered the cheerleader costumes. I've hired a YMCA basketball court and locker room facility. The story is that we're down here practicing for an exhibition home game in two weeks. You'll have twelve hours to make them look and act as American as possible."

"That won't be hard. They watch all the American Idol shows. They're all Brittany Spears, Janet Jackson copy-cats."

195

"Always nice to see the Great American Culture exported."

* * * * * *

It was nine o'clock that night when we finally unloaded the girls inches north of the border. My people were waiting at the abandoned fruit-packing platform. There was enough moonlight to see everything well. I was just about to call into the brush for my men to bring handcuffs when she let out a yell of what I can only guess was a stream of Latin obscenities and six identical black cars screeched to a halt with headlights and spotlights blazing. They pinned me in the center of their focus and I had the impulse of a cockroach in that situation. She smiled at my discomfort.

"You're under arrest for soliciting prostitution, and illegally transporting minors across a National boundary, Gringo. I'm Lieutenant Valez of Mexican Vice."

It was too funny for laughter, so I waited as my men, with guns drawn, entered the fray.

"That's nice. I'm Inspector Matt Mitchell, U.S. Immigration. We're trying to close down a gang that's been shipping girls in. We had word that you were behind it. I was sent to trap you into making a move."

She frowned. "We also received an informer's tip that a buyer was coming down and we only had to wait in the Red Pepper for him to make his move."

By the time we finally got things straightened out, badges and I.D.'s proffered and arrangements made to separate, most of the girls had slipped away. We only rounded up three and I was left to try and apologize for any mistaken impressions. I didn't question her on the lengths she'd used to establish herself as the character I might expect. Choosing not to cause me any more embarrassment, she pulled my face down and gave me a kiss to waken the dead.

"Whatever I did last night, cowboy, was personal, but I'm sent often to the border area. We might easily run into each other again, so you may want to pack an extra tee shirt."

She hip swayed her way to one of the waiting black cars.

That was three months ago and I haven't seen her since. I don't even know her first name, but I turned down a promotion that would have had sent me to D.C., choosing to stay here on the border.

#

In some cases the difference between
INLAWS and OUTLAWS is mostly
semantics.

#

# 41-NEW STARTS

"I'm going to have to let you go, kid."

"But why? Haven't I done everything you told me to? Always been your backup? Could you have faced all the dangers we've gone through together with anybody else?"

"No, but…"

"Than it's the union that's sniffing around, trying to get all us sidekicks to join for the retirement benefits. Cause you know, I always turned 'em down, always said our partnership would last, that we didn't need any contract between us, we had a handshake."

"Yeah, kid. I know, it's just…"

"What? It's just what? You can tell me, I can take it."

197

"Well, I'm trying to protect the reputation we've developed with the public. I want to quash any rumors that might start in today's politically-correct society."

"That sounds like a cop out."

"No, it's true. With the American Civil Liberties Union flexing its muscle, states passing same sex marriage amendments and public awareness of the deviate practices and behaviors prevalent, I can't take chances. Someone might get the wrong idea about a grown man who drives a flashy black car, wears purple tights, a cape, a mask and hangs around with a young boy in colored satin shorts.

So I'm afraid I have no choice but to let you go. I'm sorry, Robin, but let's stay in touch. You can twitter me anytime."

#

Maybe you didn't know, Iraqis cell-phones
work as well as American models. You just
have to carry extra kerosene to keep them
running.

#

# 42-TRUTH IN MARRIAGE

"Martha, I can't believe you lied just to get me to marry you."

"But you said you loved me, couldn't imagine your life without me. How could I know it would make a difference?"

"That was before I learned your evil secret."

"You can't mean that it mattered that much."

"How can it not? My life is ruined."

"But that's just silly."

"You don't understand how important this is to a man.   It effects my standing in the community, the way friends will look at me, point to me."

"John, you must be kidding."

"That's, that's sacrilegious."

"But you promised to love, honor and cherish me through good times and bad."

"Who could ever contemplate the bad could be this bad?"

"Oh, you're just blowing this way out of proportion."

"Easy for you to say, exposure of your ugly family secret doesn't change your whole life, your whole being, your reason for living."

"It was never a secret and I never lied.   If you'd asked I'd have told you."

"The possibility of such a thing never crossed my mind."

"But you're blaming me for your unrealistic expectation."

"You're an only child with no close relations, I had every right to assume you were the natural heir.   With a maiden name like Budweiser, how could I know you had no connection to the plant with free access to their wonderful product?   I can never explain it to my buddies. My life is over."

One difference between man and ape is
opposing thumbs.  With some men it's the
ONLY difference.

## 43-A BAD REP

That hot, humid August afternoon is still as fresh in
my memory as if it had occurred last week, not forty years
ago.  The game had ended, but I'd stayed to work on my
bat.  It's okay to roughen up the grip of a bat if it's your
own bat.  This was my own bat.  Rubbing the hard wood
with some kind of instrument gives it an even harder
surface.  I was using the sharp edge of a broken beer
bottle.  It not only performs the hardening task, but at the
same time gives it a rougher, less slippery grip.  At least
that's what the book said and I don't know if I was doing
it right, but I was trying.  As worst hitter on the team, I
needed help.  I'd been known to let the bat fly out of my
hands and sail out past third base where Mr. O'Malley
always parked his 1969 Lincoln Town Car.  It wasn't
new, but the way he kept it washed and polished, you'd
think it was.

Anyway, the rest of the team had left hours ago and
the field seemed as empty as a Texas prairie.  Using the
batting cage to support the tip of the bat, I scraped and
scraped.  When my hands began to cramp, I decided I'd
scraped enough.  Then I heard the low, menacing growl
nearby.  When I looked up and saw that it was Butch, the
terror of the neighborhood, I panicked and dropped the
bat.

Butch, a pit bull, normally chained to the Sanchez's
front porch, now stood before me, his feet spread, his

mouth agape.   Saliva dripped from fangs as big, I was sure, as a grizzly's.   The chain dragging in the dirt behind him showed the two-foot hunk of rotted portion of the porch.

I felt trapped.   I was trapped.   Chain link fence to my right, chain link fence to my left and him between the pitcher's mound and me.   Surely, after he killed me, he'd leave a few uneaten parts of my body for my family to identify.

Well, that's the way the unabridged event seemed to me at the time.   Over the years I've matured and now I remember it the way it really was.

I'm scraping my bat to give it added strength and a better grip.   When the game ended, the team had left me alone about ten minutes ago.   Using the batting cage to support the bat, I scrape and scrape.   When my hands begin to cramp, I decide the bat is strong as it needs to be. Fastening my outfielder's glove to a belt-loop, I turn toward Fillmore Street where I'll join the team at Mac Donald's for a happy meal.

As I look out at the pitcher's mound, sixty feet and six inches away, I see him.   Butch stands between safety and me.   His reputation as a vicious killer pervades the neighborhood's consciousness and even his look is off-putting.   Tucking the bat under my arm, I move toward him.   As I approach within striking distance, he licks my outstretched hand and falls in step beside me, ready, as always to share a Big Mac.

#

Be patient   I have it on good authority that by
2012 there will be a Starbucks on the moon.

#

201

# 44-AN ALTERNATIVE VIEW OF HISTORY

No one speaks above a whisper. Outside the light sounds of occasional pedestrians and the rumble of army trucks mixes with the cold wind that whistles through every crack and broken window. In here, some kind of abandoned warehouse or factory, six soldiers stand in uncomfortable disarray. The sweet clean smell of drifted snow is not enough to cover the stench of old urine, garbage, human feces and death. Abandoned military gear tells of German soldiers in the last days of the war, waiting to surrender to American or British troops and avoid the hostile invaders from the east. Also, ashes from many fires are remnants of civilians, driven from homes bombed to extinction. They had used the shelter trying to survive one more German winter. Now, the soldiers, none but the sergeant out of their teens, strip off their worn, rough, mustard colored uniforms and change into nearly new American G.I. combat fatigues, helmets and ammo belts.

"Seventeen minutes, comrades, we go," from the one in buck sergeant chevrons. "English now, no matter what happens."

The one dressed as a corporal holds back the canvas tailgate flaps of the big Dodge six-by and hands the men new M1-Garrands as they climb into the empty truck bed. The sergeant muscles open the rusty double doors that lead to a side street. As the corporal gets the engine running and starts the truck toward the opening the sergeant jumps onto the running board and pulls himself into the shotgun seat of the cab. The truck moves into light traffic on war-torn-streets. It rocks and jerks forward, but draws no attention. Just like most army vehicles, this one never did anything smoothly or without complaint. It would sway and slip, jolt and bump over a perfect surface with even the best of drivers.

"Will we make the rendezvous on time, Sarge?"

"We must, Corporal. The orders come from High Command."

"But we're not at war."

"We soon would be. And we're only doing what they tell their own Boy Scouts. How did the General paraphrase it? Oh, yes, "Do unto others before they do unto you.""

He checks the chronograph on his wrist. "Pay attention to your driving and slow down. We're 14 seconds early. We can hurry if we fall behind schedule, but if we arrive too soon we can hardly afford to linger."

The congestion on the main thoroughfare is heavier than expected, but they manage to arrive at the all-important intersection just as planned. The olive drab four-door sedan, its white flag with four gold stars fluttering from the front bumper enters from the side street. The truck hits it dead center, sending the car fifty feet before tipping it on its side and bull-dozing it another forty feet of earsplitting squeal, scraping and grinding noises like that of a thousand fingernails on a blackboard.

Inside the crumpled Plymouth, General George Patton lays in pain, still alive, but his neck broken.

The six men clamber from the truck, their loaded Garrands, ready. They search the crowd for possible hostility, but the assembling witnesses all seem focused on the mangled car on its side.

M.P.'s, already on the scene are clearing the road for the expected ambulance and other emergency vehicles. The six men move as one body through the swelling sea of onlookers. Unhindered, they head toward the Russian sector on the eastern horizon.

If you eat moldy bread every day you'll
probably never get malaria or yellow fever.

# 45-HELP

The cool spring breeze brings the scent of night blooming jasmine up to the eighth floor. It's seven P.M. and the commute traffic has stilled. The only thing of possible interest to anyone passing below might be me, Jeff, poised on the narrow ledge high above. My grip on the buildings' sooty and mildew-speckled facade is tenuous at best and my footing gives poor traction. I'm unconcerned by my unsafe posture as I look out over the rolling, pecan orchard-covered hills that stretch to the horizon. I take a deep breath and the fingers of my left hand loosen their grip as I lean out over the magnolia-lined Memphis street.

At the sound of a throat being cleared close at hand, I freeze. *Nerves.* Couldn't be anything else, I tell myself. As I recover from the surprise, my concentration returns to the job at hand.

Then from the same direction I thought I'd heard the sound, comes a soft, cultured, southern-accented male voice. "Thought it would be clear out here. It's why I waited until all the others had left the building."

I turn to stare at the man, thirty-four or so, my own age. He's wearing a well-fitted suit, now with spots of ash and dust. He too must have rubbed against the bricks. He's twisting awkwardly, looking over his shoulder at me.

*Probably been here even before I climbed out through the sticking, double-hung windows.*

On this floor, so high above public scrutiny, modernization had not taken place. The wide, high windows are still the original wavy and air-bubble glass installed when this building was the first high rise structure in forty miles. Built in 1901, it's a carryover from a slower, more peaceful time. Now it looks prehistoric among all the sleek, tinted glass and anodized towers that surround it.

"What are you doing here?" I inquire.

"I should think that's obvious as you seem to be about the same thing yourself. I'm certainly not waiting for public transportation. Anyway, I don't think the 43 bus stops on this street, not after seven P.M., anyway," He replies. "I work down on four, in accounting. My name's Mason."

"Oh, I'm Jeff. I'm, or I WAS in sales, until tonight at," I check my watch. "Seven-ten."

"Why are you doing this, Jeff? I mean I'm not usually nosey, but at this juncture, protocol really doesn't seem to matter."

"Well, a lot of things. I don't…no, you're right. I was about to say I don't like airing dirty laundry in public, but at this point I guess false modesty is useless."

"Might even help to clear your mind, ease your conscience."

"No, nothing will help."

"What can you lose but a little time? You going anyplace else soon?"

"Just seven stories straight down. Well, okay, it all started when my wife lost interest in our marriage and…me. Then when she learned that I'd lost my driver's license because I was going blind, it was the last straw. She cleaned out our bank account and ran off with my best friend. Now, since I can't drive I'll lose my job-

-after being top salesman for seven out of nine years. With a heavy mortgage I can't afford, I'll lose the house."

"Then you must be Jeff Medcaugh. Why, even down in accounting you're a sales legend. Any company would be crazy to fire you. Even blind, you'd be an asset training new salesmen."

A few pedestrians look up; see movement on the narrow ledge high above.

"Thanks for the compliment, but without any deductions the taxes would kill me."

"No, there's a new federal form1099A for anyone abandoned by a spouse. It was designed to protect single mothers left destitute, but with politically correctness prevalent today, I'd love to make a case for the reverse. Wait a minute, is your best friend, by any chance, Bud Corping from the statistical analysis division?"

"Yes, how did you know?"

"Jeff, your wife didn't leave because of anything you did. Bud's been bragging around the water cooler about an ongoing affair he was having with some guy's wife. He must have figured this was the right time to make his move.

"Why is that, Mason?"

"He's been embezzling funds and counterfeiting stock certificates. The firm just called in the F.B.I. and the S.E.C.. My evidence should have put him away for thirty years, but he won't last that long. He's sweating a dicey heart condition."

"That's some consolation. If only my own health hadn't deserted me I'd consider this…this…"

"Jeff, you say you're going blind, but you seem to see me all right."

"That's because you're close. It's only at a distance that my sight is failing. Even the new glasses are no help."

"Jeff, let me see your glasses." I hand Mason my case, he pops the lenses out and reverses them. "Try them now."

"Hey, I can see fine. In fact, a crowd is gathering down on the street. There's a very nice looking blonde in the front row. She's carrying an attaché case with the Club Med logo."

In the distance a thin siren wails.

"What about you, Mason? Why are you doing this?"

"It's a long story. I don't want to bore you."

"It'll be the last I'll hear, so try me."

"I guess. Well, for an accountant I should have kept my money in the bank, or even under the mattress, but I invested in Aquatech, the company that was to supply the world with a high-energy product. They perfected a new process for efficiently extracting protein from kelp.

They could have fed the world's population for pennies. Sound too good to be true? It is. I bought stock at forty. It dropped to five dollars just before they declared chapter eleven. The company offered me two dollars a share and I wasn't smart enough to take it. It wouldn't have mattered; I'd invested everything. I don't even have enough left for a decent burial."

I make a hard decision. "I'd better get on with this before the crowd grows larger. But I hope you'll reconsider."

I Smiled. "You have a lot to live for, Mason. You wouldn't know, of course, I only heard through an inside contact because my largest account was Trumptel, the communication giant. They've manipulated the stock of Aquatech so they can buy controlling interest for peanuts, then restructure under the name Megatrump. Your stock

207

will top out at three hundred just as soon as the news breaks."

"Great, if I could last, but I just won custody of my kids. My ex-wife didn't want them, but without capital I'll lose the apartment, I have no place to take them and medical problems of my own. This stabbing pain in my back is so bad I can't sit at a desk any longer, so my job here is a thing of short duration."

"Mason, you're about my size, let me see your shoes."

"Why? What can...oh what's the difference? I won't need them any more, here."

He hands me a pair of wingtips. One slips from his hand and tumbles past the high windows of the floors below and scatters the thickening crowd. We both see the spectators moving out in ripples, like some old Busby Berkeley movie. The shoe hits the pavement and bounces. I look inside the other shoe and smile.

"There's your problem. They're two sizes too small. Here, try mine."

I hand Mason my Florshiem loafers. Red lights flash and a wailing siren wind down as three fire trucks screech to a stop. Mason quickly tries on the loafers and smiles in total relief.

"And you know what, Mason? I've been thinking. You could move in with me. I've the perfect place to raise kids. Six bedrooms, a pool and four-car garage and with what you've been paying for rent I could swing the mortgage payments."

"Well..."

"And if your ex reneges, we could claim that we're gay and adopt them. With the permissive nature of society today it would have to be accepted."

"By, God! Jeff, you are ONE HELL OF A SALESMAN. I'm feeling like a winner already. Let's give it a try."

As the men struggle to reopen the recalcitrant window between them, the THU THU THU THU sound of heavy rotor blades comes over the horizon. A huge blue helicopter zooms into sight and from a uniformed figure comes a booming authoritative voice.

"Don't worry down there. We're the police and we're here to help you."

With the chopper hovering directly above, the downdraft of its powerful beating blades is too much for the two men trying desperately to maintain their fingertip holds on the rough surface. Below, firemen scramble vainly to position their large, framed canvas jump nets and the crowd cries in horror as two figures, blown off the narrow ledge hurtle to the pavement.

#

Iranian laptop computers are as efficient as the best from the western world, as long as someone turns the hand crank fast enough.

#

# 46-GAINING TIME

It's near midnight, the bow dips, the swells crest and the foredeck is awash. Any seaman unlucky or unwise enough to try to navigate any part of the superstructure would now be taking advantage of interactive swimming lessons.

These two-stackers are familiar with forward travel in washboard fashion, but with the big warships surrounding us, we simulate a marshmallow trying to stay afloat in the center of a downspout. Riding a washtub over Niagara Falls might be easier than staying atop these waves.

The roll and pitch are bad enough, but we must stay alert for danger when a prolapsed stomach is the most immediate danger most of us can contemplate. With running lights out and silence the order of the day we creep southeast. Well, it <u>feels</u> like creeping and full-ahead break-neck speed at the same time. War emergency conditions dictate that all personnel stay no further than five meters' distance from their combat station and within hearing of the Captain's orders.

This week, my family will be making holiday plans for dinners and sharing time with loved ones seldom seen during the rest of the year. It's extremely unlikely, yet I pray that I might be home in time to enjoy the season with them.

Although, on wartime footing a normal thirty-day tour of sea duty will surely be extended under these conditions.

Its late December eighth, a day no one will remember, when the call comes to initiate the attack. Then, as we cross the date line and we lose a day, it becomes the morning of December the seventh, nineteen forty-one. We prepare to launch planes for the strike that will assure us a glorious victory over the American Imperialists. Maybe at least their Hawaiian outpost will remember this day.


#
No apologies to the Beatles, but Belief in
Yesterday is no great shakes. Having faith in
tomorrow shows character.
#

# 47-UNLIMITED POWER

I'd waited over an hour in the Secretary of Energy's outer office and shown my I.D. and security clearance to a phalanx of security guards who photographed me for the name badge I must wear at all times. It read Bruce Wincott. When eventually I was admitted to the inner sanctum, I had to show, for the seventh time, my credentials as an professor of Geological and Terrestrial Anomalies at Stanford University on sabbatical leave before the latest guard would even make eye contact. The case at my feet was shown no more interest than the cup of coffee I held.

Carefully, I lifted the amazingly shiny, black rock from the case. It's smaller than a grapefruit but weighs over sixty-five pounds. I set it atop the two-inch thick rubber pad I'd spread on the corner of the desk. His assistant entered and watched with ill-disguised suspicion. Secretary Hoffner was perfectly at ease, but showing his open hostility.

When I placed the six-volt lantern battery beside the rock and prepared a connecting wire to the positive terminal of the battery, they sneered. Touching my multi-meter's two probes to the rock, the meter, as expected, showed no charge. The battery read, with no surprise, 12.1 volts D.C. Touching the single wire from battery to rock caused no visible difference. Now, however, the battery showed zero voltage. I watched their eyes as I once again tested the rock. It read 60.5 volts D.C. They stared, wondering how the trick worked; they knew it couldn't be what they'd seen. I waited for them to voice their response. As I waited, I took one of their own 100-watt bulbs from a credenza's desk lamp and holding it by the glass part, I fastened an alligator clip to the screw base and touched the other end of the single wire to the rock. Dimly, but surely, the bulb lit.

"This bulb requires 120 volts of current. I'm giving it only half that amount and it can't be sustained for long, but notice that I need not complete a circuit. Normally we'd need two wires for that." As the lamp gradually lost illumination, they came closer, unconvinced; yet willing to learn the barroom trick. They touched all the items, assuring that there was no possible way for what they had just seen to have happened. While they did their little hands on "we know it's fake, but how?" bit, I took a power inverter from my case and plugged it into the wall outlet. Its dial read A.C. 120-volts.

"Now I'm going to plug a single wire into the positive output. This will give me 12 volts direct current converted from alternating current."

I touched the single wire to a different spot on the rock. Again there was no visible change. When I metered the rock, though, it registered 600 volts D.C. Handing asbestos gloves to the two doubters, I drew a small gear-driven motor from my case. As I unplugged the inverter and touched the single wire from the input of the motor to the rock, I explained that they were free to hold the exposed motor shaft, to try to keep it from turning. The torque of this motor, while turning at less than it would be at high speed, they were unable to stop the spinning arbor. I removed the wire and let them grip an arbor at rest. As soon as I again made electrical contact, they lost traction.

I finally had their complete attention. Uninvited, I sat, smoked a cigarette and waited, comfortable for the first time since I'd entered this building.

"This phenomenon has been repeated hundreds of times with current increases to over twelve thousand volts.    It only works with D.C., but that's easily converted to A.C.."

I let the smoke curl around my crew cut head and smiled at their disapproval.

"I propose to establish a circuit of these Wincott Generators across the country running from San Francisco to Charlotte.    From them we can power the entire continent for three cents of every dollar now being spent."

With no words to form intelligent questions, they just stared as I repacked my equipment and prepared to leave.

"I'll wait twenty-one days for your answer.    Within that time, I'm willing to conduct a more professional presentation to any consortium of federal agencies or engineers who wish to view this miracle wave of the future."

"I'm not sure we can move that quickly.    We need time to properly discuss this among ourselves."

"Take all the time you want, Secretary Hoffner. The first of next month I'm presenting this to Canada and if you don't move faster than normal bureaucratic turtle speed you can buy energy from the north country at only fifty cents on the dollar.    Still better than the billions you're spending on nuclear plants and all those other losing propositions, like wave action, geothermal, wind, and solar panels.  They all work, but combined you can't produce 40% of the energy you need.   I can give it to you and show you a 100% payback within the first six months of operation."

I picked up my case and left.   I knew I'd be under surveillance, but I'd planned well.    Once part of the crowd within Washington D.C.'s fast rail system I'd be lost to followers.

It didn't take them twenty-one days.    After two more demonstrations, they agreed to my demand and

213

deposited the one billion dollar down payment to my Swiss account. Naturally, they'd tried unsuccessfully to learn the source of my magical rock. But only I knew that it came from the meteor believed to have caused the elimination of all the dinosaurs on earth.

That may well be, I'm not a paleontologist. I only know that the one piece of lodestone I'd found after three years of excavating was capable of producing the results I had promised. Now all I had to do was find about seven more tons of the stuff somewhere.

#
Some people say that as you grow together you start to look like your dog. How do you think that makes your dog feel?
#

# 48-KNUCKLEHEAD

*South Central Idaho-Wednesday Evening*

The roar of the tuned exhaust of almost a hundred horses is muffled by the snow that hangs on the thick air of the high desert as the white blanketed Harley passes the highway sign, U.S. 93-Jackpot 1 mile.

*Southern Nevada-Thursday Morning*

The bright chrome work sparkles in the dawn's light and the dark blue metallic fenders and tank glisten like a thousand fireflies as Bret pulls the forks onto the Las Vegas Strip.

At the Sundown Motel on Mohave Drive, he carries his two fitted saddlebags into his assigned room. Before crashing on the queen-sized bed he wedges rock pitons into the top and bottom of the single entry door.

## *Las Vegas-Thursday Afternoon*

Shaved, showered and dressed in clean casual clothes he looks younger and more like a bull rider entrant to the P.R.C.A. than a society playboy. He's neither. Nor is he as young or innocent as he looks. Out on the Strip, he flags down a cab to take him to the Winner Casino's main entrance.

A valet welcomes him with a smile and open hand. He ignores both, strolling purposely to the Special Events Desk.

"John Butcher, Falls Church, Virginia for the Poker Tournament."

The woman smiles half-heartedly and points to the double staircase leading to the mezzanine. "Upstairs, first right."

He takes the steps two at a time and is confronted by a pair of uncaring self-involved employees busily reliving private fantasies. They frown at his interruption.

In unison…"This is a private tournament."

"That's why I'm here, slick."

He fills in his name, Karl Baker, Chapel Hill, North Carolina on an enrollment form.

The two stare, doing little to hide their assessment that he doesn't belong here. "There's a twenty-five thousand buy-in and a minimum hundred thousand credit line."

Not allowing them to waste anymore of his time, Bret shows them a bank draft. "I'll pay in the morning, when I get my table assignment."

He leaves the casino and walks a circuitous route to the alley behind The Sundown Motel. Backing onto the common alley is the Eventide Motel. He checks in as

Marvin Grey, Tampa, Florida.    With key in hand, he returns to the Sundown Motel and walks his Harley across the alley to the parking lot of his new accommodations. He doesn't check out of the Sundown.

## Las Vegas- Thursday Afternoon

Artie, the Casino Manager and Carlo (Eastern money behind the Casino), have watched Bret on a security monitor.   Their gaudy cravats and gauche pinky rings mark them indelibly as nuevo-rich.

Artie frowns.   "He's a last minute entry."

"You said the fix was all set."

"It is.   The house players know when to go all in, lose, clap their heads, mumble and collect their guarantee on the way out."

"So who's this new guy?"

"I don't know, I'll check."

Artie takes the short corridor to the closed circuit T.V. monitoring room, whispers to Eldon, a fat, balding man eating his second Big Mac.

Eldon, through huge mouthfuls says,  "Computer's got nothin' on him and he's not in the "do not admit" pool and the other casinos got nothin' to share.   He ain't known in Atlantic City, Reno or Laughlin.   Not no other place neither."

"Well, go through his room and see what you can find."

"He's not registered here."

"He just walked in from the street?"

"No, camera shows him arriving by cab.   I can check with…"

"Do it."

The trace takes just enough time to allow Eldon to finish his third mega-sized fries and second chocolate shake.   "None of the cabs have him coming in from the

216

airport and he's not a guest at any other casino in town. As soon as he registered for the tournament, he left by foot."

"Well, he's gotta' be tracked by I.R.S."

"Not unless he wins. That's why they only keep agents on hand during play."

Eldon reads the screen.

"There's no such person as Karl Baker in Chapel Hill, North Carolina. He's got no driver's license or Social Security number and no such person ever filed North Carolina or federal income tax returns."

Artie wrings his hands. "Make sure security notifies us the minute he's back."

"Could be he's a N.G.C. plant."

"Yeah, in which case they won't let him lose his entire stack before makin' their move.

## Las Vegas-Friday Morning

Bret enters the casino and receives his participant package. It entitles him to a four star champagne buffet breakfast in the main dining room. Instead he pays cash for black coffee and a dry bagel at the stand-up deli. The activity is such that wearing dark sunglasses, he manages to slip past the initial surveillance detail unnoticed. Taking his assigned seat, he eyes his competition and is eyed in turn; the dealer explains house and tournament rules and the players are given chips for their buy-in amount. The constant, dull murmur of TV cameras and the gallery activity interrupt an otherwise near-graveyard silence.

Artie scans security monitors nervously. "We got his table assignment?"

"Yeah, boss."

"And the cameras got a good shot of his hands and face?"

217

"Yes and no. He keeps his head down. We never get a clear shot of his face.

"We're still good. Our sensors will defeat him just like all the yokels who think they can beat the house."

Bret is in the number six position at table 26 when Marathon Texas Holdum begins and the first hand is dealt. Without looking at his hole cards, he goes all-in. The uniform gasp around the table turns it into a diorama. Naturally, his play is greeted with a great amount of anguish, but after surreptitiously checking their draws, each mumbling player passes. Bret pulls in the pot. It's nothing to brag about, consisting of only the ante and bet amounts from one round, but it does start this game off with a **boom**.

Nadia, the stunning redheaded cocktail waitress takes their orders. She floats, as if she doesn't even need the incredible legs that seem to reach forever. She brings Bret bottled water, and their eyes flash acknowledgment of an unspoken bond. Everyone else at the table is drinking beer or cocktails; Bret doesn't open his water.

Bret obviously forces the action by raising on the pre-flop. It implies that he is either being dealt a strong button every time, or he's a fool, but no one can spot his tell-sign. He wins twelve of the first twenty hands, including all the large pots. During a break, he carries his bottled water to the bathroom, empties it and refills it with tap water.

Artie flushes, "What do you mean you're not reading his cards?"

Eldon cowers before his computer screen. "He catches them in the air, doesn't let them hit the table. Our sensors can only read the cards if they have clear access. It's like line-of-sight radio transmission."

"Well, after he lays them down, then."

"No, sir. He always keeps one hand underneath his cards."

"That makes no sense. Who the hell does that?"

"He does, sir. It's almost as if he knows about our sensors."

Bret, in fifteen minutes, wins the first table and brings the odds down from six hundred to one, to two hundred to one. In two hours at the next table, he wipes out three players. Each time Nadia brings drinks, her eyes manage to find him. Three hours later, he's cleared two more tables and climbed to seventeen on the leader board. He has only to win at two more tables to reach the finals.

Carlo glowers at a quivering Artie. "How the hell can he get this far so fast?"

"Security cameras confirm his every move. He's not getting signals or using an electronic device. We've switched his table position, so even if he had a confederate, it wouldn't help."

In the final round of the day, Bret faces the best players in the country and is way over his head, yet retains a slight advantage. These five have played each other for decades. Acutely aware of his unorthodox strategy and aggressive betting should allow them to outplay him. If he continues the same technique, they will, but the others almost trip over their own tongues saying "all-in." He passes the first hand and Bud DeGraff, trying to mimic Bret's tactic, loses his entire buy-in. Three pots later, Skinny Boile tries it, Bret folds, the pot goes to Trucker Hoss, and the table is reduced to four. When Bret raises by forty-five thousand, Sammy Detter calls and Bret sees his two queens improved by a flop with two aces. At the river, he gets the third queen and raises one hundred seventy thousand.

219

Artie Grips Eldon's thick neck with an iron hand. "Whenever that redheaded floozie flaunts by, his eyes shine and I swear she stands a little straighter. Get her in here."

"But Boss, in eight hours she hasn't said a word to him, brought him a drink or made eye contact."

"Well, something's going on. I'll use her to get him gone."

With the subdued lights of the casino, Nadia's ermine-trimmed, black sequined outfit draws the attention from her long, spectacular, copper-colored hair that it deserves. However, under the office overhead lights, it's clear that dressed in anything she'd never be mistaken for a boy. She stands erect before the casino manager and waits to hear the reason she's been summoned.

"How long have you known the guy drinkin' bottled water?"

"If he's ever been in here, I've never served him."

"How come you know who I'm talkin' about? You musta' served a hundred bottled water drinkers."

"No one's ever caused a stir like the man you must be referring to. Everybody in the gallery is talking about him. They're laying bets on whether Jack Falco will take him. And if he wins it all, the local TV will do a special on him."

"Yeah, well, I want you to cozy up to him."

"I can't do that, sir. Nevada and tournament rules prohibit it."

"I'll think of some way around that. You just stick close to him."

"Yes, sir. May I return to my station?"

He hands her something. "Keep this pager with you at all times, in case I want to get a hold of you."

All eyes follow as she floats back to the tournament. Artie whispers to Eldon, "Stay with her. If this guy makes a move, I want her guiding him."

## Las Vegas-Friday Evening

The television broadcast of the finals is scheduled for Saturday night, but the game has progressed too quickly, and might well be over tonight. Normally, they'd just record it for delayed broadcast, however, with Pay-Per-Vu over-subscribed, FCC watchdogs keep an eye on everything. Artie is forced to call a recess. He announces over the P.A. that all participants are comped their suite, meals and all hotel facilities. Bret moves with the other players toward a queue at the hotel desk. Following at a distance, Eldon, with a tight grip on Nadia's elbow, guides her, whispering in her ear. Her eyes grow large as she hears what she's expected to do.

Bret moves to the casino cashier. The woman behind the iron grate calls her supervisor for help; he solicits the head cashier's assistance. They all try to dissuade Bret from removing his earnings. When he insists, they fill a carry-on vinyl case with his two million, seven hundred thousand winnings. With the extra grand prize of ten million still available, they assure him that, until conclusion of play, his cash is safer in their vault. He thanks them, hefts the cash-laden case. Nadia seems to accidentally fall in beside him as he reaches the elevator. Her smile warms the atmosphere of the otherwise empty car they share to the twentieth floor.

As they exit, her arm is in his and her leg makes contact in a very familiar way. At room 2020, she takes his key-card and fits it in the slot. As they enter, he slips his arm around her waist, holds her and kisses her. Without moving from her side, he shuts and locks the door, turns on the lights and says, "Take off your clothes."

Her heart leaps. "Hey, I'm not a hooker. I just had to keep you occupied and learn what I could about you. I went along with that, but I never…"

"Take off your clothes. You can use the bathroom if that makes it any easier."

To her frightened look is added a confused frown. She comes out a few minutes later wrapped in a thick bath towel. Below, she's still wearing the black leather boots, but above, only warm-glowing, satiny skin shows.

Without giving her the lecherous look she's expecting, he brushes past her, and stuffs her sequined costume into his cash-swollen gusset bag. Keeping her within reach, he rips the telephone from the wall, then, maintaining eye contact, he explains her only option. "If you wait twenty minutes before raising an alarm, I won't have to tie and gage you. If, as you say, you're an innocent victim, you can explain you had no choice, I shanghaied you."

"You're cutting out? Not going for the big prize?"

"They'd never let me win that and if they did, I'd never get out with it. No, I have more than I came for."

"They won't just wait for you to turn up at the table tomorrow. Once they learn you've withdrawn cash, they'll guess your plan."

"Can't be helped. As soon as I'm out the door, start counting. You promise to wait twenty minutes?"

She nods, solemnly. At the door he turns for a last look at her, then he's slipping down the empty hall as quietly as possible. Seconds later the door of 2020 opens and Nadia, with one glamorous leg showing says, "Hey, cowboy, how far will you get if I chase you screaming RAPE?"

222

"Why are you doing this? I never meant to hurt you."

"You're signing my death warrant. They'll never believe I didn't help you and since now I know they'll try to kill you, they'll never let me live."

"I could have knocked you out or tied you up and made a clean get-away."

"But you didn't. You still can if you come back and we talk."

He's caught in-between. He can't make it to the elevator and if he rushes the door she can slam and lock it in his face. He shrugs and slowly returns to the suite. She closes the door behind him.

"I can get you out of here, but you have to take me with you. That's not a bad deal; I'm an asset, not a liability."

His slumping posture indicates that his solo plan has just become a duo. Still wrapped in the towel, she leads him to the maid's closet. Finding a white servant's jacket for him, she slips into a starched maid's uniform. She shows only a flash, changing between towel and uniform, but the unfettered body revealed is better even than the sequined costume promised.

"Put your money case in this laundry hamper and push it to the service elevator."

He's quickly into this new order of things and the two, seemingly, going about housekeeping chores, take the elevator to the basement. Passing the maintenance shop she directs him to the end of the corridor. They're almost free, but a guard at the employee entrance glances up from his paper. She waves, takes Bret's arm and makes the universal two-finger V gesture, indicating they're going outside for a cigarette.

The guard nods and goes back to reading.   Outside, she smashes the pager and dumps it in the trash, then motions him to reject the white jacket and take his bag.

They easily gain the four-acre parking lot and he guides her, slalom fashion around hundreds of cars, to the southeast corner.   Out of range of security cameras, they cross the street and casually walk the eight blocks to the Eventide Motel.   He's packed and ready to go.   He drops an envelope with cash for his checkout in the after-hours slots at both motels.

He frowns at her.   "Now what?   How will you explain your failure to keep me in tow?"

"Are you kidding?   Going back would be suicide."

"So what will you do?"

"I have to get out, leave everything behind.   Well, I don't have that much to leave."

"Do you have any money?"

"A small bank account that now I can't get to."

"I can cover that part.   How will you go?"

"Hitch hike.   I can't buy a ticket.   That would leave a trail."

"Well, if you don't mind wind in your face, you can ride behind me."

She stares into his face, trying to read his thoughts. When he doesn't blink or break eye contact she makes her decision.   "I guess we could try that."

Packing his winnings into his saddlebag, he hands her a spare crash helmet.

Posing in his loose-fitting denims, she does a few model pirouettes for him.

"Sexy, huh?"

His grin holds no hint of disappointment.

He kicks the bike into the low rumbling idle and shows her where to place her feet.   She's already figured out where to put her hands and they take the back streets to the highway.

## Central Nevada-Saturday Morning

Dawn breaks in the eastern desert as they pull into a small roadside café, an emblem of a bygone era. Over breakfast he tells what she wants to know, but can't find a way to ask.

"Three years ago, my father retired from the Air Force. He'd built counter-surveillance systems for the latest fighters, but he loved best ferreting out invasive electronic technology. His expertise at verifying slot payouts saved the Nevada Gaming Commission millions by catching crooked casino owners."

She listens intently, while sliding a new leather belt through the loops that allow her to regain her hourglass figure in his bulky male ranch outfit.

"He always finished his circuit in Wendover. Then one night, passing the Texas Holdum Parlor, his sensor detector picked up a weird reading. Later, he mailed his explanation of the scam in a letter to me. He knew he'd been followed and was in danger.

His body was found the next morning out in the desert. The autopsy said natural causes due to exposure. The police never questioned why he was there, or how he got there."

Outside, she twists her mass of hair into a coil, fits it into the crash helmet and stalls, wanting to hear the rest, not wanting to ask.

"This same Holdum Tournament Outfit pulled-up stakes the next day, even though they'd contracted for another week.
I couldn't prove they killed my dad, but I traced them here where they'd bought the Winner's Casino. Now

225

they'll need to explain my winnings to the money people. I expect they'll soon be eating Nevada sand."

Several truckers take notice of his bike. "Nice lookin' hog ya got there."

Bret grins. "Thanks, it's a '47 Knucklehead, left behind when we bought our ranch. My dad and I rebuilt it from scratch. It took us three winters, but it turned out kinda' nice."

Back in the saddle, she wraps her arms around his waist and whispers into his ear,

"I don't need the two hundred thousand you offered. I'd rather try Idaho ranch life with you."

"Well, in that case, it's a good thing I saved your sequined outfit. It's how all well-dressed Idaho ranch wives dress.

#

Women _always_ win because they argue with
only one man. Men _never_ win because they
must argue with ALL women from the
beginning of time.

#

226

# 49-THE CIMARRON KID

The old lady squinted red-rimmed, beady black eyes at the fire that seemingly unnoticed, sent smoke and sparks in her direction. Hunched over her cup, she drank scalding; hot brown liquid that one can only assume is coffee.

How has she managed, in this God forsaken country, to survive to the age of…what? She looks a hundred, but is probably no more than sixty, I wondered. Well, if she's old enough to remember the story, Liberty Magazine will pay me half a cent a word to get it. I'll bring them an eyewitness account of the Cimarron Kid's exploits, one of the most famous, and perhaps the last of the notorious southwest killers. He…but that's her story, so I'll let her tell it.

She hunkered down into what had to be a most uncomfortable position and sucked smoke from a clay pipe, nested easily in the channel made by the missing three teeth below and two above. I held pencil and pad ready.

"He was starvin'. Not 'cause there wasn't 'nough food, it was so he'd get the idée. His pap figgered it was time for him to move on. Said 'Fourteen's when a man ought to be fixin' fer hisself'. Wasn't like he'd be missed at school; his learnin' was on the farm and the school marm was his pap an' he taught with a twelve foot bull whip, not no book an' writin' slate.

He walked away carryin' only a rusty knife and a waterskin; wearin' the same ragged clothes he slept, worked, and fished in. You might understand it's hard to sneak up on game when they can smell ya a mile away. So he lived that first week on corn too moldy to feed ta hogs. His first break come when he lucked onto a

227

nester's cabin. The man was workin' in the field and the missus was down by the crik washin' clothes. He ate everything he found in the cabin and when the missus started back, he snuck out the side and took the wet clothes she'd left to dry on the cottonwood branches. Downstream he got his first bath since the last spring rain.

Dressed in his new duds, he worked west, toward a town he'd heerd tell was off thataways. He din't find no town, on'y some loose, broke horses grazin' on sparse desert grass. Them horses was so old they could'a died standin' up and you'da never knowed it 'till the wind tipped 'em over. Catchin' one, he led it to a rock so's he could climb on. It wasn't good enough ta sell, but it got him to a scrawny settlement of about six thousand, if you counted the five-thousand fleas in that census. He begged a job at the livery stable and got grub, a loft to sleep in an' three cents a day. It was startin' his career off with a bang, an' that proved to be prophetic when a crew a trail drovers pulled in to drink and have a look-see at the local feminine talent. That consisted o' the bartender's fifty-year old, two hundred pound wife. I guess sellin' rotgut at a nickel a shot don't pay a man what he thinks he deserves, so his wife made the climb to the sleepin' rooms ten or twenty times a night."

She tamped out her pipe and filled it again from a rawhide pouch.

"When a couple o' the drovers couldn't wait they turn it was settled with six-guns, leavin' two dead and the rest too drunk to care. The kid picked saddle and tack from the pile and exchanged his wore out ol' plug for a better nag. Ridin off. he felt' like the world was his'n. With his feet in stirrups and a horse able to travel at more'n a mile a hour, he was able to drive some loose beeves into a mesquite draw where he tied the feet of one and carried it over his saddle horn to a near-by buncha starvin' reservation injuns. They waren't particilar 'bout brands, nor proof o' ownership. They give him a dollar Mex and three paira' moccasins; even let him share some stew. That calf had been slaughtered an' cooked most while the blood was still apumpin'. When the drovers tracked the missin' hoss to the injun camp an' saw the moccasin tracks they figured it warn't worth chasin a dead man's mount, and they quit they search. This gave the kid his first real break and with the next stole calf; he found a ready sale at a trade-post. They give him a old .44 Remington and a pair o' regular boots. He din't have no holster and the gun was so wore out that the bullets tumbled. Made the God-auffulest hole in a man you ever did see. It later 'came his signature, but that wasn't 'till he'd improved his personality. His method o' makin' friends was to get someone drunk so's he could steal whatever they had. He'd not really developed the taste for killin' yet and he considered it Christian-like to allow a man to keep his scalp while only losin' goods that could be replaced.

The first time he tried it was in a bar down by the border. He met a Mex with a powerful thirst, an' a purty gun, silver trimmed holster an' concho belt. By the time the Greaser was out an' the kid could steal the fancy trappin's it was near sun-up. He was miles into the territory afore he realized the gun belt was too short and the hogleg was a nickel-plated .36 caliber, too small for serious work. So he kept his Remington and swapped the Mex outfit fer a smooth workin' trapdoor Springfield and a hunderd rounds. There warn't no scabbard fer the rifle, so he tied it with a rope and hung it over the horn. That worked okay 'cepten' when he had ta travel at a axcellerated pace, like he offtimes did."

She scooched' up closer to the fire and curled her legs under herself like as if she was winding up a spring, ready to uncoil at any minute.

"That problem was soon fixed when he run onto a bunch o' cowpokes eatin' beans 'n bacon at a small campfire. They saw the iron he was packin' an' 'vited him to set a spell and 'joy some vittles. He dasn't refuse, as he hadn't eaten for mor'n a day. 'Sides, they looked like the kind useta pokin' cows belonged to other folks without they knowin' 'bout it. They wounta taken kindly to his ridin' on through, him knowin' they's whereabouts. He was right in his assessment of the moral caliber of this bunch. Over a cup o' boilt coffee he reconized several as bank and stage robbers.

Tyin' up with that bunch was the high point in his edjacation. He just held the horses at the first bank they chose to make a withdrawal from. It's lucky for them they din't trust him not ta mess things up inside, 'cause him bein' <u>outside</u>, is what saved they hides. A nosy sheriff come sniffin' 'round the corner and the kid saw him first. Sheriff went down with a keyholed chest wound. They stuffed it with a towel, but it din't do no good. He sent a bunch other interferin' lawmen and clumsy self-taught gunslingers to their last rewards, but that first was the one he was proudest of."

She gestured for me to add some more mesquite branches to keep the fire going. I did, anxiously, knowing that I'd likely never have a second chance at an interview like this. She was so old and brittle; she'd probably be dead before this made it into print. I figured I'd have to help her back to her sod-covered lean-to.

"At first he put his faith in that six gun or the Springfield, but he never really hit his killin' stride 'till he learned to rely on that old knife he brought from his farmin' days. He worked on it with rawhide and oil 'till it was sharper than any razor some citified barber would use.   He kept it in his sleeve and practiced till he could slide it out and slit open a grainsack faster'n your eye could follow.   A couple ex-gang members learned not ta kid him 'bout his sod bustin' roots.   He could cut the buttons offen a pardner's shirt and never draw blood.   By just stretchin' another inch he left at least ten non-pards watchin' they life's blood drain away.   He never got credit fer them killin's cause there was no tell-tale signs left, like with the ragged hole them sidewise .44 bullets left, but I guess he'll have to content hisself with the history you write 'bout him."

I didn't want to embarrass her with my viable doubts.  I accepted her detailed recitation, but if I couldn't verify her role as an actual observer, my editors would never buy an unsubstantiated eyewitness account.   I needed corroboration, so I asked.

"Just how were you able to obtain this intimate biography?   Are you implying that you have your knowledge first-hand or did you get it from another source?"

I didn't see her move; it was just a blur, intermingled and indistinguishable from the fire smoke.  I only realized what had happened when I looked down at my shirt and vest, both open, laying my chest bare.   I watched her resettle herself into that coiled spring position and carefully refit the knife into her sleeve.   Her lizard-textured face split in a gap-toothed smile.

"Cause I is him."

#

I'm an only child.   So is my brother.

#

231

Bellflower, California 1971

The delivery van has just left and their grandmother's belongings are piled on the walkway leading to the guest bungalow where she'll soon be living. The girls, siblings, Carla 13 (she says 13 ½) and identical twins, Roxy and Rosie, 12 (they say 12 ½) look at each other with unspoken questions. They obviously mean well, carrying the bundles in for her. Their efforts are complete, except for the heavy box of books. It splits apart within feet of the target coffee table. The one item that draws all eyes is a scrapbook with *Gina* in red nail polish across the front. (Now it's not documented whether it fell open of its own volition or was helped by thirty inquisitive fingers).

Each volunteer manages to hold a corner of a yellowed newspaper article describing the Santa Barbara earthquake of 1941. They read of the devastation of hundreds of homes and the disruption of families. Noted is the mention of their family name among those dislocated.

Carla, the natural leader in her mind, voices their unanimous thought.

"Should we ask her?"

One of the twins responds first, (it's impossible to tell which, as they are indistinguishable and have the habit of answering for the other and completing the other's sentences, to completely confuse and annoy).

"We have to, it's…"

"…our filial duty…"

"…you mean familism."

232

"Whatever gets us there…"

"…they both mean…"

"…essentially the same…"

"…thing."

Among the items not purged automatically from the broken carton is an exposed, fifty-foot reel of movie film. (Now there's no question about this item. It didn't fall out or otherwise burst upon the world. The girls had to dig to find it, but find it they did).

Silent thought descends upon the trio, but not for long. In near unison comes:

"Mom's got an old movie thingama…"

"jig, a projector. It's…"

"…up in the attic."

They meet at the doorway and try to stuff three bodies through an aperture meant to accommodate one at a time. Finally, they reach the attic above the three-car garage and by dint of being tallest, Carla reaches the rope that lowers the accordion-type ladder. She also elects herself as the one to find and retrieve the Bell & Howell 8mm projector.

"Plug in the…"

"…dohickey…"

"and let's…"

"…watch it."

The twin most mechanically minded, loads the film and in the semi darkness, they watch the action unfold on the garage wall.

Revealed is a beach party with teens running, flirting, roasting hot dogs over an open fire. In the foreground, a lovely young girl, is recognized, from mantelpiece photos, as their grandmother, Gina.

"Turn up the…"

"…sound, we can't…"

"…hear what they're…saying."

Carla, in the role of moderator, says,

"There is no sound.   It's called a silent movie."

"Hey, we're…"

"…surprised they…"

"…even had cameras in…"

"…those days."

The twins move up as close as they can get and squint at the images.

"How can we…"

"…tell what…"

"…they're saying?"

The action is halted as three minds go into deep concentration.

Carla is the first with an epiphany.

"Mrs. Murphy, down the street."

"She's deaf and…"

"…she reads…"

"…lips.  Good…"

"…thinkin'"

"…sis."

They troop, arm-in-arm to the neighbor's house. With a little cajoling, they enlist the help and expertise of Mrs. Murphy.   In concert, they watch the rewound epic film.  Mrs. Murphy translates.

"Her brother and his friend have just arrived in a brand new Packard convertible.   Her brother has gone off girl hunting, leaving her on the beach.   She's alone for only a minute or so when this other boy, Mario, attaches himself to her side.   She's trying, unsuccessfully, to reject his advances.        You can see here, without warning, he kisses her.   So here's where the real dialogue begins."

*You know I hate you.*
*I know.*

*So why did you kiss me?*
*It had to be done.*
*We've known each other since kindergarten and you've never done that before.*
*I know.*
*Why?*
*Why do I know?*
*No, why did you never do it before?*
*The time wasn't right.*
*So why did you do it now?*
*The time was right.*

"He kisses her again."
*You did it again.*
*I know.*
*Well, stop it.*
*What?*
*Kissing me.*
*Why?*
*Well, because, just because.*
*Doesn't sound like a good reason to me.*

"He kisses her again, this time with his arm around her waist."
*I told you not to do that.*
*Do what?*
*Kiss me.*

"He kisses her again, this time with both arms around her."
*That!*
*What?   You said kiss you and I did.*
*No, I meant…*

"He kisses her again."
"You can see other couples climbing the stairs to the cottage, probably looking for bedrooms.   She takes

Mario's hand and pulls him toward the waterline. Then, something happens, the camera is shaking, kids are falling down, others are running and then I think the camera is dropped onto the sand because the film goes dark."

## PART II

"Are we going to tell her?"

"She'll be home before mom is…"

"…off work, let's get her…"

"…out in the gazebo. We'll say we…"

"…want to have…"

"…tea."

"Yeah, she loves afternoon tea and those little Russian teacakes. Also, we can cut it off if mom or dad arrive."

"How will we explain that we know what we know?"

"Here…"

"…she comes…"

"…now."

"You two get the tea and stuff going and I'll get her talking."

"Nuh-uh,…"

"…not without"

"…us."

"I just meant about her shopping trip. I'll wait 'till we're all together to hit her with the real stuff."

A very attractive woman over thirty (and that's as close a guess as I'll make) enters, drops two armfuls of shopping bags. The girls are seated around the gazebo table. Gina switches her interest from one to the other according to which one of the twins is speaking. She's too smart to call either by name, as there's never a way to tell which one will answer. She just throws a question or response out there. Small talk is made until the tension within the teens is about to burst, but when they have the tea and fixings and all are seated around the awninged, redwood gazebo. The time is ripe; the girls can wait no longer. They blurt out their inquisition.

"Grandmother, we…"

"…thought we would…"

"…help you unpack."

"And we came across this scrapbook."

"We didn't mean to…"

"…snoop, but we did, and…"

"…now we have…"

"…to know."

"Who was this Mario and what happened between him and you?"

Gina smiles in complete comfort at their curiosity.

"Why, I haven't thought about that in…25 years. It was the beginning of summer, nineteen forty and one and we were living in Santa Barbara. I'd just turned fifteen and was, let's say, in full bloom. I'd had a crush on Mario since the fifth grade, but he never noticed me. He and your uncle Carlo were best buddies, but they were always doing boy things. When they finally got around to noticing girls, I was a day late and a dollar short. That's why I said, and thought, that I hated him."

"But what happened with you and Mario?"

"There was a huge earthquake. Places were sliding off the cliffs into the sea. Nobody knew what to do, but when the shaking quit we all ran for home. Our house was just a pile of splinters. The next morning, with what little we could salvage, we moved to Fresno. I never saw Mario again. I learned that his family home was wiped out, just like ours. They moved, but I never learned where. I expect, that like your uncle Carlo, he was killed in the war."

"Okay, so…"

"…did you too…"

"…ever…do it?"

Carla, with a shocked look,   "That's an incredibly indiscreet thing to ask."

Gina blushes.   "Oh, I don't mind answering.   It's kind of sweet, actually.   No, but he told me he loved me and wanted to be with me forever."

Silence, as teen brains fashion new interrogatories. Finally, Gina saves them the trouble.

"I finished high school at sixteen and met your grandfather at the packing plant where we both worked. We married and had twelve fine years.   When cancer took him, I felt the loss.   He was a good man, just not demonstrative or emotional.   He lacked Latin passion."

"Certainly not like it would have been with Mario, I'll bet."

"No, nothing like that."

"So grandmother, he's been gone for years now."

"Why haven't…"

"…you found…"

"…somebody new?   You're in your…"

"…early 40's, incredibly attractive, in…"

"…phenomenal health.   Surely you…"

"…must still have your…"

"…juices flowing."

"Yeah, you just decided to sell your place in Sherman Oaks and move in here with us 'cause you were lonely.   But it can't be the same as having a man of your own."

## PART III

The three teens are again seated in the gazebo with tea and cakes ready.   All that's lacking is Gina.   Her new

Corvette pulls into the driveway and the sound of her high heels echoes off the Spanish tiled entrance. The first view of her is the perfectly coiffed auburn hair with burgundy waves that swoop down over one eye as a bird gathering energy for flight. The girls are already in anxiety overload. Carla is the first to speak.

"Grandmother, please join us for tea."

Gina, in conservative cut but revealingly tailored raw silk suit, ruby red blouse and matching shoes, eases her way onto the clean, waiting, canvas director's chair. The luau torches and citronella candles combine with the scent of night blooming jasmine to create a most romantic setting. Gina clearly loves these three, but always suspects them of some kind of skullduggery and is seldom wrong.

"Grandmother, we found your Mario on Microfiche at the library."

"What?"

"We got his last name, Francotti, from your old yearbook.

"Didn't get a good look at him though…"

"…only good picture was the swim…"

"…team photo, but those…"

"…bathing trunks…"

"…were out of the…"

"…dinosaur era."

"All except that head of hair."

"And we learned that…"

"…unlike your guess, he…"

"…isn't dead."

"He married in nineteen forty-seven and it only lasted a year and a half. He never remarried or had any children. He's lived in Redondo Beach all this time."

"He has a…"

"…very successful real…"

239

"…estate business there."

Gina holds herself in compressed emotion, allowing neither her breath, nor her feelings to escape. "And I suppose you think I should drive down and renew an old acquaintanceship?"

"Well, yes…"

"…and…"

"…no."

"He's waiting in the living room to see if he's welcome."

"You don't. I mean, I couldn't, I shouldn't. He's really here?"

Carla uses a flashlight to give the pre-arranged signal. In less than a minute the door from the main house opens and silhouetted by the living room light, a figure moves slowly toward them. Slowly, but confidently, not hesitantly or reluctantly. In the dim torch and candlelight, he's revealed as a man of medium height. The dark green polo shirt and tight jeans enhance his slender, but athletic build, but the lasting impression is the full, luxurious, wavy mane of white hair. Gina rises to her feet as if on an air-filling balloon. She seems awed, but not nervous, as if this is a scene she's relived in her mind thousands of times. Without a word, Mario moves to her and without warning, kisses her. She responds.

"You know I hate you."

"I know."

"So why did you kiss me?"

"It had to be done."

"We've known each other since kindergarten and you've never done that before."

"I know."

"Why?"

"Why do I know?"

"No, why did you never do it before?"

"The time wasn't right."

"So why did you do it now?"

"The time is right."

He kisses her again.

"You did it again."

"I know."

"Well, stop it."

"What?"

"Kissing me."

"Why?"

"Well, because, just because."

"Doesn't sound like a good reason to me."

He kisses her again, this time with his arm around her waist.

"I told you not to do that."

"Do what?"

"Kiss me."

He kisses her again, this time with both arms around her. And her arms slide around his neck and pull him into a kiss that would be a minimum PG 17 even in a Disney movie.

## PART IV

Just kidding. There's no part four. You have to make that up for yourself.

#

You're getting very sleepy.   You can hardly hold your eyes open.   You hear only my voice.   It's best that you pull over and park.   You can't keep your eyes open. You're feeling good.   You're feeling better than you've ever felt before.   It's all because you bought this book. You will continue to feel this good if you buy my next book.

Don't listen to the clerk who might say he doesn't carry my books.    Demand that he stock at least a thousand copies as you and all your friends want to buy, BOOK 3-"HEADS OR TALES."

While selling electronic equipment, I built my connection with manufacturers into an audio recording business. Later, looking for a pet for our two small sons led to the breeding and showing of Beagles. That and field events led to the experience of following Bloodhounds in police searches.

During long winters at Lake Tahoe, marathon reading gave me the idea of trying creative writing on my own. Following college courses, writer support groups and open mike performances honed my short story style and response to my BLOG resulted in incorporation of over three hundred stories (the Times News called them "bizarre.") into this series of five books. Vaughn Phelps

# V. I. P.  Publishing

P.O. Box #911
Twin Falls, Idaho 83303-911

# ORDER FORM

Date:

Ship to:

Quantity        @$11.00 Each        Total

     Short, But Sweet

     Short, Not So Sweet

Postage

Postage $3.00 for one or two books, .75 cents each
additional book

Enclosed Check/Money Order for:        $